THE WRONG PATH

Amish Romance

HANNAH MILLER

Tica House
Publishing

Sweet Romance that Delights and Enchants!

Personal Word from the Author

To My Dear Readers,

How exciting that you have chosen one of my books to read. Thank you! I am proud to now be part of the team of writers at Tica House Publishing who work joyfully to bring you stories of hope, faith, courage, and love.

Please feel free to contact me as I love to hear from my readers. I would like to personally invite you to sign up for updates and to become part of our **Exclusive Reader Club** —it's completely Free to join! Hope to see you there!

With love,

Hannah Miller

VISIT HERE to Join our Reader's Club and to Receive Tica House Updates:

https://amish.subscribemenow.com/

Contents

Chapter One

The gravel crunched beneath Mary's feet as she trotted down the dirt road, nearly a mile from her quaint Amish home shared with her mother, father, and younger sister Susan—all of whom had called it night.

But hers was just getting started.

She picked up her pace, sweating beneath the thick green dress she and her mother had sewn two months before. Mary fanned herself as she jogged and sighed in relief as she rounded the corner to the end of the road. Amber and Denise were already waiting for her in their small pickup, flashing their high-beam lights as she approached. She wiped the sweat from her brow beneath her *kapp* and gave her *Englischer* friends a small wave.

"Hurry up, Mary," Amber called, leaning out the driver's side window. "We've been waiting for almost thirty minutes," she added, as the cool night breeze tussled her bleached hair.

"I'm so sorry," Mary said sheepishly, as she climbed into the backseat. "My *dat* was holding me up. I had to help with the garden."

Denise snickered in the front seat, her tanned knees pulled up to her chest. "You mean *dad*, right?"

"Right," Mary nodded, clicking her seatbelt in place, swallowing hard. "Dad." She had yet to fully catch on to a lot of the *Englischer* words, and despite her new friends' willingness to take her under their wing, they seemed to pick fun more than she'd like—but maybe she was just being sensitive. After all, the *Englischer* kids teased each other often, and no one seemed to take much offense.

"I heard there's gonna be a lot of boys at the party tonight," Denise said, spinning around to gaze at Mary, as she pushed a lock of stray dark-brown hair behind her ear. "Are you excited? You should let your hair down tonight."

"Mmm," Mary murmured, giving her a shy smile. "I'm not sure." She shrugged, trying to play off the nerves rattling her chest. Even though she had begun to socialize outside of the Amish community, she had yet to cross those lines—though she couldn't help but be curious. Amber and Denise wore a lot of make-up and always had perfectly styled hair, often paired with tight jeans and short tops that showed their stomachs.

Mamm would kill me if I wore something like that.

"Oh, come on," Denise pleaded, sticking out her bottom lip playfully. "Just one night—and I brought my make-up, too."

"Maybe just tonight." Mary sighed, reluctantly, as she pulled her *kapp* off her head, revealing her blonde hair. She loosened the perfectly knotted bun, allowing her hair to fall in waves to her waist.

I'll put it back up before I return home.

"Yay," Denise squealed, clapping her hands together. "This is perfect."

"All the guys are *so* curious about Amish girls." Amber caught Mary's eye in the rearview mirror, raising her eyebrows playfully at her. "You should talk to them more."

"I don't know..." Mary's voice trailed off as she gazed out of the truck's window into the blackness of the night. So far, she had avoided the *Englisch* boys at all costs during her *Rumspringa* adventure and hadn't planned to change that. Besides the fact that they made her nervous and were a bit rowdier than she preferred, she was also courting someone.

"You can play the field you know," Amber said, her tone turning more serious as if she had read Mary's mind. "You're only young once—and there are a lot of guys out there."

Mary pursed her lips, her mind running back to Isaiah, who she had begun courting only a couple of weeks prior. She had always had a crush on the tall dark-headed man, but he had long kissed *Rumspringa* goodbye—not that he had ever seemed to be very interested in it from the beginning. She shifted uncomfortably in her seat. He wouldn't like anything about what she was doing.

"It's just for fun," Denise added in response to her silence. "It's not like it has to mean anything. Besides..." She shrugged. "You might find us *Englischers* are a lot more fun."

And sinful.

"We'll see," Mary said, forcing her tone to be light and playful. There was no sense in arguing with the two of them—and maybe they were right.

She glanced out the window into the blackness of the night as Amber drove down the back roads. There wasn't much to make out in the darkness, and even though Mary had gone out with Amber and Denise a handful of times now, her heart still pounded nervously in her chest while riding in a vehicle. They just went so *fast*.

So much faster than a buggy.

Her mind raced with the photos she had seen of car crashes and other vehicle accidents. Her cousin, Grace, had been severely injured in a buggy accident a few years back, and Grace still walked with an odd limp. Mary forced herself to take a deep breath, swallowing the fear she felt in her chest.

I'm fine.

Gott *please take care of me.*

Chapter Two

This is awful.

Mary coughed, choking down the beer Amber had given her an hour earlier. Nothing about the taste was satisfying, but everyone around her seemed to be enjoying it. She scanned the crowd, searching for her two friends, but couldn't spot them. They were at an *Englischer's* house, though she had no idea *whose* house it was. Regardless, it was a big house with a pool—something she had never seen in person before. The girls wore bathing suits that were terrifyingly immodest, and she blushed in embarrassment just at the thought of putting on something like that.

"So, you're Amish?" a slurred voice said behind her.

Mary turned around, her eyebrows raising as she took in the blonde-headed boy, probably about her age. "I am," she said, drawing out her words with a cautious tone.

"You're missing your bonnet thingy." The boy motioned to the top of his head, his eyes wide and bloodshot.

Mary nodded, shifting uncomfortably. "I let my hair down this evening," she said, her voice sounding forced. She had never been one to feel awkward around her peers in the Amish community, but this—this *Englisch* world was a whole new experience.

"It's pretty," he slurred, shooting her a smile that left her feeling jittery. He was a handsome boy, though very different from the boys at home. He was in a tight t-shirt and his arms were covered in black ink—tattoos. He was what Amber and Denise would call "hot and fit."

Mamm would hate him.

And that thought alone spurred a sense of guilt—but also excitement.

This was playing the field.

"Thank you," Mary said, doing her best to give him a warm smile back.

"What's your name?" he asked, having to yell over the ever louder hip-hop music playing in the background of the night.

"Mary," she shouted back to him.

"I'm Jerrod." He winked at her, and Mary blushed in response. "Do you need another drink?" he asked, eyeing the beer in her hands.

"*Nee*, thank you," she replied, shaking her head.

That's the last thing I need.

"Wanna dance then?" he asked, stepping closer to her, and her heart sank.

Maybe I don't want to play the field.

The song switched from a hip-hop song to a slow soft much quieter song, and Mary exhaled sharply, glancing around her, wishing more than anything that Amber and Denise would show back up and rescue her from having to dance with this drunk *Englischer*.

"Come on," he pleaded, before pouting playfully at her.

Mary swallowed hard. "All right," she sighed. It was just one dance—right?

"Sweet," he shouted, grabbing her hand and dragging her out into the backyard where other couples were swaying to the music. He pulled Mary into him, placing his hand at the top of her waist, and she felt her chest squeeze.

But it wasn't in excitement.

It was in pure shame.

She swayed back and forth with Jerrod and did her best to think about anything other than what was going on around her during that moment.

There was no need for her to feel guilty, was there?

Rumspringa was all about experimenting and determining her place in the world. When her friend Beth Miller was in *Rumspringa*, she had chosen to leave the community and marry an *Englisch* man.

But I have Isaiah.

What would he think of me dancing with Jerrod?

Her stomach churned with sickness at the thought of him finding out about such a thing—another man with his hands on her waist, in a way that Isaiah had never even come close to doing. She glanced up at Jerrod, whose eyes were closed, and whose mouth was mouthing the words to the song playing clearly through the speakers. He wasn't even paying any attention to her, and though she really didn't want to be dancing, it still was disappointing.

As the song ended, Mary backed away quickly, breaking loose from Jerrod's grip. She caught her breath as Amber and Denise came into view, giggling in the corner of the backyard. Sighing with relief, she walked toward them, but a hand caught her wrist, spinning her around.

"You leaving me so soon, Amish girl?" Jerrod said, a crease in his brow.

"Sorry." Mary smiled sheepishly. "My friends are waiting on me, actually." She pointed to Amber and Denise, before they waved at her.

"Oh." Jerrod's voice turned a bit whiny. "Well, I'm sure they'd understand you hanging out with me a bit longer."

"I have to get home soon," Mary said, twisting her hand from his grip. "I'll see you around though."

"Right," Jerrod quipped. "If that's the truth and you're not just avoiding me... We'll be having another party down by the river next Friday night."

"Mmm," Mary said, drawing in a deep breath. "I might be here—I'll have to ask my friends. They pick me up for the parties," she added. "Plus, you've been drinking, so..." Her voice trailed off as she gazed at his dark green eyes.

"I'll make sure I'm not drunk," he said, narrowing his eyes at her. "And I'll pick you up for the party."

"I should probably have Amber and Denise pick me up," Mary insisted.

Jerrod sighed, but went silent, obviously studying her. "I'll see you then," he finally said as Mary slipped off to join Amber and Denise.

"Ooooh." Amber broke out in a smile as Mary approached the two. "Jerrod was *so* into you. He totally likes you."

"He's been drinking too much," Mary pointed out, crossing her arms across her chest.

"So?" Denise shrugged. "I don't think that matters."

Mary bit her lip. "I think it's time for me to get home."

"It is getting really late." Amber sighed, glancing down at her cell phone. "My dad's home tonight, so I better not push my luck."

Thank you, Gott.

Chapter Three

Mary blinked her eyes, and stretched her arms above her head, noticing the sun shining fully through her bedroom window. Her back ached on the firm mattress beneath her, and she groaned as she sat up groggily. Rubbing her tired eyes, she stood, rolling her shoulders. Her eyes fell to the window, and she squinted out beyond the backyard. Her stomach knotted.

Oh, nee.

Nee, nee, nee.

Her younger sister, Susan, and her father were already hunched over and working in the garden. Hurriedly, Mary dressed and ran through the empty house, blowing past her mother hanging laundry on the line.

"Mary Yoder," her mother scolded. "You slow yourself down before you plow somebody right over."

"Sorry, *Mamm*," Mary called as she continued her jog out to join her father and sister. She rounded the corner of the house, and as her father looked up at her, a weed in his hand, his eyebrow arched.

"I'm so sorry, *Dat*," Mary huffed, struggling to catch her breath.

"Your *mamm* said you got in late," he replied gruffly, his tone unreadable, but his dark brown eyes were filled with disappointment.

Mary's gaze fell to her shoes. "I'm sorry, *Dat*," she said, swallowing the lump in her throat. They allowed for her to partake in *Rumspringa*, but that didn't mean that they liked it —or that she didn't feel guilty about it.

"We've already been out here for almost two hours," Susan snapped, looked vexed. "Not all of us get to run around and party like you do."

"Susan," their father's voice came out as a warning, and Mary shot a glare at her younger sister, who gave one right back.

"*Ach*, come on, then." Susan rolled her eyes. Mary cringed at her sister's words—she sounded just like Amber and Denise.

"Start plucking the weeds," their father directed, clearly ignoring the tension building between them.

Mary nodded, and immediately began the task of pulling the grass and weeds that had begun to sprout up between the rows of vegetables and herbs in their large garden. She was careful to shake the dirt from the roots, before tossing the unwanted vegetation into the cart that had been pulled up and parked along the border.

The three worked in silence, and Mary let out a sharp exhale as her handful missed the cart for the second time in a row. Huffing, she walked over, picking the weeds up from the ground.

"Are you hungover?" Susan asked, her voice low. At sixteen, Susan was getting old enough to catch onto things Mary was involved with—and clearly she was picking up on the lingo of the *Englischers*.

"*Nee*," Mary snapped, before adding. "You have to stop talking like that, though."

"Why?" Susan retorted. "You talk like that all the time."

"But I'm nineteen," Mary shot back, her tone stern.

"And I'm sixteen," Susan mumbled, rolling her eyes before returning to the other side of the garden to pick more weeds.

Mary's shoulders sagged in the heat of the mid-morning sun, sweat rolling down her face. Her head ached, but it wasn't from the little bit of alcohol she'd consumed. It was from the fatigue.

And guilt.

Dancing with Jerrod had turned out to trouble her much more than she'd intended it to. A lot of Amish dabbled in such things during *Rumspringa*—some did a lot more than just dancing.

But it still didn't feel right.

"Hello there, Isaiah." her father called from behind her. Mary froze, hearing the creak of a buggy becoming louder as she was bent over, plucking a large spiny weed from the soft soil.

So far, their courting had only consisted of a couple of buggy rides. Isaiah had been nice, and Mary had been attracted to him for a very long time.

But it was *Rumspringa*.

And there's nothing wrong with playing the field a little.

"Mary," Susan nudged her, a weed in her hand. "Isaiah is here."

"I heard," Mary said before standing up, her head growing a bit light from the heat and change of position. Her eyes met Isaiah's bright blue ones, and something stirred in her chest, but she swallowed it. His wagon was filled with the lumber for the barn addition her father was scheduled to start soon.

Her eyes followed him as he hopped down from the wagon and helped her father unload it, a few pieces at a time. They stacked the lumber carefully on the ground, up against the north side of the barn. Mary tried her best to ignore them, continuing to pluck weeds, but her eyes kept falling on the muscles flexing in Isaiah's shoulders and arms as he unloaded and carried the wood.

"He's so strong," Susan muttered, standing beside Mary.

Mary didn't respond to her sister's comment, only huffed out a sigh in annoyance—though Susan was right. Isaiah *was* strong. Her mouth went dry at the thought.

I need some water.

She shook her head, and walked toward the cart, tossing another handful of weeds and grass toward it. They thudded against the side, before falling to the ground.

Missed again.

Grimacing, Mary made her way to the cart, careful not to step on any of the tender young vegetables. She kept her eyes on the small pile that had missed the cart and bent over, reaching down to grab it up. Just as she did, a larger hand appeared, plucking it up from ground. She jerked upward; her eyes immediately being met by pale blue ones.

"Hello, Mary," Isaiah said warmly, before tossing the wad into the wagon.

Mary automatically smiled at the deep voice greeting her. "Hello," she said, her voice quiet as she held his eyes.

"How's the weeding going?" he asked, looking past her to the garden for just a second before his gaze returned to hers.

Mary wiped sweat from her brow, feeling the gritty streak of dirt she was sure she had just smeared there. "It's going." She grimaced.

"Here." Isaiah chuckled, reaching out to wipe the dirt from her forehead.

Mary's cheeks flushed with heat, as she gazed up at him. "Thank you," she mumbled. Isaiah was a lot taller than the *Englisch* boy she had danced with last night.

I danced with an Englisch boy last night.

"I have to get back to the shop," Isaiah said, his eyes studying Mary's face. "But I thought maybe I could take you on a buggy ride Friday?" he ended with the last bit coming across as a question.

Mary bit the edge of her lip.

That's the night of the party.

"I..." she began, her voice trailing off. "I have plans Friday night with my friends," she said, her voice quiet as she looked from Isaiah to her father and sister continuing their work in the garden.

"Ah." Isaiah sighed, his shoulders sagging. "You're awfully busy these days," he added, his voice thick with disappointment.

"I'm sorry," Mary said, continuing to avert her eyes. "Maybe next week I'll have more free time." She brought her eyes back to his face, pained by his hurt expression.

Isaiah nodded. "I guess I'll see you at the youth singing next week, and we'll talk then."

"*Jah,* I'll see you then." She forced a smile, giving him a small wave as he returned to the wagon.

Ugh.

Part of her wished Isaiah would leave her alone for a while so she could enjoy the rest of *Rumspringa* in peace with her new friends, while the other part was consumed with the gnawing guilt of her conscience. She scowled and returned to the garden, ignoring the curious look written all over Susan's face.

Chapter Four

"I saw Isaiah stopped by to drop off lumber for the barn addition," Mary's mother began as they waited for the biscuits to finish baking.

"*Jah,* he did." Mary sighed, eyeing her mother. Usually, her mother was a rather quiet woman, but when it came to her daughters' love interests, she was anything but. Ever since Isaiah had shown interest in courting Mary, it seemed to be all she ever wanted to talk about. Susan had drawn the eye of one of the Stein boys, too, and her mother seemed to linger on the subject with Susan more often than not.

"The two of you are courting, *jah?*" Her mother was studying her, and Mary looked away, casting her glance back to the oven.

"I s'pose." Mary shrugged. The last thing she would be telling her mother was that she was playing the field—or that her *Englisch* friends suggested it.

"Mary?" Her mother placed her hand on her shoulder, and she looked up at her, her mother's green eyes mirroring her own. "I thought you were fond of Isaiah. You've spoken so highly of him for years."

"I..." Mary's voice trailed off, as she carefully considered her response. "I do think highly of him, *Mamm*. It's just," she paused again, unsure of how to continue. "I don't know. I have a lot happening right now."

Her mother pursed her lips, her eyes narrowing. "You mean, you're busy running around with those *Englisch* girls, *ain't so?*"

"They're my friends." Mary's brow creased, her tone growing defensive at her mother's prying tone. "They just happen to be *Englisch*," she added.

"Hmm. I thought Grace and Anna were your friends?"

"They are." Mary paused, thinking of her two childhood friends. Grace was married and Anna was engaged to be married at the end of summer—neither had spoken to her much in a couple of months. "They seem to be busy with their own endeavors."

"They've both been very blessed," her mother said, her tone seemed to be a bit chiding.

Annoyance rattled in Mary's chest. "I s'pose so."

Her mother sighed heavily. "I don't want you to give up something *Gott* has blessed you with because you are deceived by your worldly friends."

"*Mamm*," Mary groaned. "*Rumspringa* is a part of our tradition. Everyone gets to experience it, and I didn't even partake until this summer. I'm just being a normal teenager."

"You are becoming very well-versed in the *Englisch* ways, and I was hoping you wouldn't," her mother said, before pulling the pan of biscuits from the oven. "Especially with Isaiah's courtship. You know…" She sat the pan down, before turning to Mary. "You can turn away from the *Englisch* world whenever you so choose."

"I know that," Mary snapped, folding her arms, before letting out a breath and purposefully relaxing her shoulders. "I don't want to talk about this anymore."

Mary's mother returned to prepping the meal with another sigh, but didn't say anything more, much to Mary's relief. It wasn't that Mary didn't like Isaiah—but there was just so much excitement beyond the confines of their small community.

Like pretty clothes.

And loud music.

And cars.

And cool friends.

Mary felt the apprehension rising in her chest as she continued to help her mother fix dinner, thinking about the upcoming Friday night. Amber and Denise had made it clear that they'd all be going, and Mary should, too—and that Jerrod would be one of the 'hottest' boys there. Both had urged her to pursue him, but Mary had made it clear she wasn't interested in him.

But he is handsome.

Although not as handsome as Isaiah.

Mary bit her lip as she carried the bread to the table for supper, her mind falling back to Isaiah's hurt expression when she had turned down his offer of a buggy ride Friday night. Guilt churned in her stomach, and she recalled the first time Isaiah had approached her with the prospect of a buggy ride. She had been beyond excited and flattered—but that was before she had met Amber and Denise.

This is my only chance to see the world beyond our community. Isaiah has already had his chance at such things.

Except he had hardly participated in anything. Isaiah was devoted to the Amish church and community, much more than a lot of his peers. Most of the elders respected him for that, and the fact that he was following closely in his father's footsteps in running the lumberyard.

Most girls would love for him to court them.

Her heart sank. Maybe she should've found a way to go for buggy ride before the party. She felt torn; she wanted more than anything to fit in with her friends and experience the fancy world—but she also didn't want to hurt Isaiah and miss out on what *Gott* wanted for her life.

Maybe after Friday.

Just one more night won't hurt anything.

Chapter Five

Mary sat on the edge of her bed, wringing her hands, anxiety causing her fingers to be laced with sweat. The week had passed faster than she had expected, and it was Friday. Hardly able to stomach her supper, she had only picked at the chicken her mother had fixed.

"Where are you going tonight?" Susan peeked her head into Mary's bedroom, her hazel eyes wide.

"None of your business," Mary retorted, raising an eyebrow. "You don't need to know such things," she added, her tone remaining stern. The last thing she needed was for Susan to be picking up on more of her outings.

Hurt flickered in Susan's eyes. "Why won't you just tell me? You used to tell me everything."

Mary's chest tightened. "It's best you don't know," she said, keeping it short. In all reality, it was to protect her younger sister rather than shut her out, but she knew Susan wouldn't understand.

"Are your new friends taking you?" Susan continued to pry, stepping all the way into the room.

Mary sighed, running her hand along the light blue quilt on her bed. "They are—*jah,* but it doesn't matter."

"When can I go?" Susan asked, her voice eager.

"Next year," Mary replied. "But I doubt I'll still be going to such things by then."

"So then why go now?" Susan's brow furrowed. "I don't see the point."

"Because it's *Rumspringa.*"

"But you don't *have* to keep going," Susan pointed out, her voice laced with confusion. "I don't see why you do."

Mary shook her head in frustration, standing up from her bed. "Just leave it be," she said, tired of the questions she didn't have the answers for. "I have to go, anyway."

"You usually don't leave this early—it's barely dark," Susan said, crossing her arms.

"They're picking me up early," Mary said, squeezing by her sister as she slipped from her room. Thankfully, Susan didn't follow her out of the house. Amber and Denise had promised to pick her up a bit early so Mary could change clothes—and they had moved their meeting place to less than a quarter mile from home. Mary took in a deep breath of the Pennsylvania air, shutting the front door behind her softly. She didn't want to disturb her mother and father, who had both retired for the evening.

From the porch, she could make out the headlights just a little way down the road, and her heart picked up with anticipation.

"Where are you going tonight?" a deep voice asked, startling Mary, causing her to jump sideways, grabbing onto one of the porch railings for support.

"Isaiah," Mary said to Isaac who just so happened to be standing a few feet away in the yard. "What are you doing here?"

"I came to drop off the nails your father needed." He held up a bucket, before walking to the porch and setting it down. "I had to run a load of lumber to the Millers, so I decided to drop them off tonight, so he'd have them for the morning."

"That was kind of you," Mary said with a smile, though her eyes were still focused on the lights shining behind him down the road.

He nodded, before turning to look at the headlights himself. "So, where are you going, tonight?" he asked the question again, turning back to Mary.

"I'm hanging out with Amber and Denise," Mary said quietly, averting her eyes from his. She knew he would be hurt that she had chosen them over him—but she didn't want to *see* it.

"Right," he said, his tone flat. "Is that them?" He motioned to the headlights, which seemed to suddenly be moving in their direction. Mary gritted her teeth.

Please don't come closer.

"I guess that's why you couldn't go on a buggy ride with me this evening," Isaiah said heavily.

Mary forced herself to finally look up at him, meeting his eyes. "It was," she mumbled, caught by the hurt she knew would be there. "But it had been planned before you asked me on the buggy ride," she added quickly, hoping to ease his disappointment.

It didn't work. Isaiah shook his head, his eyes cast down at the ground.

"I'm sorry," Mary said, biting her lip in frustration.

Why did he have to show up now of all times?

"Is someone else courting you?" he asked, his voice low and tense.

Mary's heart dropped. "What do you mean?" she asked, knowing exactly what he meant, but afraid to answer.

He raised his head, meeting her eyes. "I mean..." He paused. "Are you seeing any of the *Englisch* men that you hang around? I know those men are curious about Amish women," he added, his voice flat and firm. "Beth Miller even ran off and married one of them."

Mary swallowed hard, thinking back to dancing with Jerrod. "I..." Her voice trailed off as a black SUV pulled up right in front of her house, positioning itself so that it was hidden in front of the small patch of trees, not far from the barn. However, that didn't prevent the headlights from casting across the yard, illuminating the two of them.

"Just tell me the truth, Mary," Isaiah demanded, his voice strained as his eyes stayed focused on Mary's face—despite the opening of car doors and music booming into the quiet of the evening. "Please," he added, with a hint of impatience.

Mary held his gaze, still debating on whether dancing was the equivalent of *seeing* an *Englisch* man.

"I danced with a boy, but I didn't like him," she said, her voice in a near whisper. "It didn't mean anything at all—I promise," she said, her stomach growing nauseous as Isaiah squeezed his eyes shut tightly.

"Come on, Mary," Amber called from behind them, standing just in front the SUV in a pair of cut-off jean shorts and a short black top. Mary knew the outfit would show off her pierced belly button.

"You better go," Isaiah said, never even casting a glance in Amber's direction. "I have to get home." He walked toward his horse and wagon parked just a little further up the drive than the SUV.

"I'm sorry, Isaiah," Mary said, her chest tightening.

Chapter Six

"Who was that?" Amber asked, as Mary trotted to the SUV, her head still spinning from the conversation that had just taken place.

"My friend," Mary said quietly, heading for the backseat of the car.

"He's cute for an Amish guy," Amber cooed, climbing back into the passenger seat. "We have Denise's car tonight. My truck has a flat," she added.

"It's a nice car," Mary said, her mouth feeling dry as she slid into the backseat. The seats were a smooth black leather and cool to the touch.

"Hi." Denise smiled, turning around to see Mary. "We brought you something special for tonight."

"Here," Amber said, handing Mary a paper bag stamped with a logo she didn't recognize.

"What is it?" Mary's brow creased as she held the bag in her lap.

"Look inside and see, silly," Denise said playfully, motioning to the sack. Both of her friends waited, their faces eager as Mary opened the sack to view its contents.

She pulled out a pair of jeans and small blue t-shirt with ocean waves on it. "Are these for me?" Mary's eyes widened as she held the clothes.

"Yes," Amber and Denise both squealed in unison.

"Thank you," she said, her tone full of shock and excitement. "I'm not sure if they'll fit though," she added. "And I've never worn jeans before."

"We guessed," Denise said, a large grin across her slim tan face. "But I'm really good at estimating sizes."

"We were going to get you shorts," Amber said, leaning on the center console. "But we thought you'd be more comfortable in jeans."

"Thank you," Mary said again, fingering the clothes.

Englisch clothes.

Despite feeling excited by what her body might look like in such clothing, she also felt that familiar pang of conviction pulse through her chest. She glanced out the window to where Isaiah's wagon had been parked, but he was no longer there. Mary had been so caught up in the new gift she hadn't even noticed him leave.

"We'll take you to the gas station so you can change in the bathroom," Amber said, as Denise pulled away, heading back down the dirt road toward town. "Or you can change in the backseat."

Mary gulped. "Change right here in the car? Umm. *Nee.*"

"I brought make up, too," Denise added. "We're doing you *all* up tonight."

The gas station they pulled into was at the very edge of the Amish community, just off the main highway. Denise whipped into a spot right out front, and Mary got out with her sack, heading for the entrance. Both of her friends followed her inside to the bathroom at the very back.

Mary shut herself into the biggest stall at the far corner of the ladies' room and tugged her dress off and over her head. Her heart pounded as she pulled the jeans and shirt from the bag, looking them over again.

I won't look Amish in these.

She pulled her feet out of her heavy black shoes, deciding to try on the jeans first. They felt rough on her skin, clinging to her legs in an unfamiliar tightness. Surprisingly, Denise had lived up to what she had claimed—they were a perfect fit. The dark jeans sat just below Mary's belly button, and as Mary ran her hands over the denim, she realized how pronounced the curvature of her hips and slender legs were in them.

These are tight ... and inappropriate.

Mary sighed, considering the idea she could just take them off and tell Denise they didn't fit. But that would be lying.

She glanced down at the hem of the jeans, cuffed just above the top of her shoes. It actually looked good—really good.

Just for tonight.

Mary shimmied into the t-shirt, and as she pulled it down, she was surprised to see it fell just below her chest. She tried to pull it down further, but there wasn't enough material to make it to the top of her jeans.

One of those short tops.

She swallowed hard. The shirt was worse than the jeans, showing off her flat stomach—though she didn't have a piercing like Amber.

I should take it off.

Mary picked her pastel green dress up off the floor, gazing down at the soft cotton material in her hands for a few moments. Her heart pounded in her ears as she studied the perfect stitching down the side.

"Does it fit?" Denise called from outside. "We're dying to see you."

"*Jah*," Mary replied shoving the dress into the sack, before swinging the door of the stall open.

"You look *amazing*," Amber squealed. "Look at that hot bod you've been hiding beneath that dress."

Mary felt her cheeks flood with heat, before noticing herself in the mirror behind her two friends. She caught her breath as she took herself in. Her chest seemed larger under the material, and her pale stomach was out for the whole world to see.

I look just like them.

Except for my kapp.

"Time for makeup," Denise chirped, pulling a small cosmetics bag from her purse.

Amber removed Mary's *kapp*, and Mary asked about the object sitting beside the sink, already plugged in. A curling iron, Denise told her.

Denise busied herself applying makeup to Mary's face, and Mary quietly observed her quick strokes in the mirror, creating a very dark eye and applying a dark red lipstick. Amber picked up the curling iron and quickly added more waves to Mary's blonde hair, and as they stood back, admiring their creation, Mary couldn't help but stare at herself in amazement.

I don't even look like me.

"You look absolutely stunning," Denise exclaimed.

"Thank you," Mary replied, her voice shaking. Did she look stunning?

"Let's go party," Amber said, ushering them out of the bathroom, and back through the store. Mary followed the two girls outside, her arms wrapped around her mid-section, doing her best to shield her now-viewable stomach from the rest of the world.

It's just for one night.

Chapter Seven

The party at the river wasn't quite as big as the one the previous week at Jerrod's house, but it was still crowded. Mary felt as though all eyes were on her as she followed Denise and Amber around, careful not to spill her red cup of 'punch' that had been poured for her. After just a sip, it was clear that it was less fruity and contained copious amounts of alcohol, burning Mary's throat as she took small sips.

"I love the river," Denise slurred as the three girls stood in a semi-circle, gazing at the moon glinting on the water. Some of the teens were brave enough to splash around in it, but most just stood around on the banks, dancing and laughing, as loud music boomed through the night air.

"What's up, ladies?" Jerrod appeared, shouting over the loud music. His gaze fell straight on Mary, and she shifted uncomfortably from one foot to the other under his scrutiny. The look in his eyes as they traveled over her made her stomach churn.

That has to be a sin in itself.

"You look gorgeous," he said, drawing in his breath sharply. "You're the hottest girl here," he added, his eyes meeting Mary's again.

She didn't blush.

The only thing she could feel was the conviction eating away at her for wearing clothes that brought such attention to her body.

"Hey," Denise snapped, slapping his muscled arm playfully. "We made her that way."

"Yeah, sorry." Jerrod shook his head. "You two are beautiful, too, but man..." His eyes were still on Mary. "She is something."

"Thanks," Mary said, her voice a bit flat. The attention was unwanted—and she knew Jerrod was practically drooling over her.

He doesn't even know me.

"You know there's another one of your people here though," Jerrod said, his voice light and casual.

What? Who?

"You mean Amish, right?" Denise asked, her eyebrows raised. Mary remained silent—frozen by the thought of *whom* could possibly be at the party.

"Yeah, over by the fire with Roger," Jerrod replied, shrugging.

"I need to go find them," Mary said, panic rising in her chest.

What if it's Isaiah?

"Whoa," Jerrod called after Mary. "Wait."

Mary ignored him, taking off through the crowd, noticing a few of the boys rough-housing and throwing punches down by the river's edge. The sight made her even more nauseous, and she dumped the punch out of her cup, tossing the cup into a trash can. As she headed toward the fire, her eyes scoured the people around her for any sign of Amish.

Isaiah is going to be so mad at me.

She wrapped her arms around her bare stomach, silently preparing herself for the lecture he'd give her once he saw what she was wearing. Swallowing hard, Mary pushed through a couple of drunk girls, babbling and laughing amongst themselves.

Why did I ever think I liked this?

Mary stopped just short of the campfire as shock flooded her.

That is not Isaiah.

That's Susan.

Completely forgetting about her attire, Mary rushed across to the see Susan, who was leaning on a short dark-headed man. He appeared to be around Mary's age, which only enraged her further.

"What are you doing here?" Mary demanded, and Susan's head jerked in her direction.

"I c-c-climbed in the back of that car when your *friends* got to the house," Susan said, her voice slurring slightly.

Mary was mortified as she noticed the empty red cup in her sister's hand. "How many of those have you drunk?" she asked, unable to disguise the fear in her voice.

"I dunno." Susan shrugged. "Why do you have to be worried?" she slurred the last syllable, before playfully punching Mary in the arm.

"We *have* to go home," Mary said, reaching for her sister's arm, ignoring Roger's raised eyebrows.

"So, you're Amish, too?" he interrupted.

"*Jah*, she is," Mary snapped, looking around for Denise and Amber, who she thankfully pinpointed as they seemed to be headed right for them.

"You don't *look* Amish," Roger added, his eyes running up and down Mary's body again.

Mary gritted her teeth, ignoring the urge to punch him right in his large pointy nose.

"Can you guys take us home?" Mary called, as Amber and Denise approached.

"Who is this?" Amber asked, ignoring Mary's questions, her brow furrowed.

"This is my younger sister, Susan," Mary said, unable to hide the irritation and shock from her voice.

"Cool." Denise smirked. "How old is she?"

"Sixteen," Mary answered for her. "Can you *please* take us home?" She didn't care whether she was able to hide the desperation from her voice now.

I just need to get my sister home. And never do this again.

"We just got here," Amber answered, folding her arms across her chest in a stubborn pose. "I'm not going home yet. Your sister will just have to hang."

"Yeah," Denise added. "She'll be fine."

"I really need to get her home," Mary pleaded, fighting to swallow the lump growing in her throat.

"There's Derrick," Amber said quickly, ignoring Mary's request. "We'll catch up later," she added, quickly squeezing Mary's arm before trotting off to a tall red-headed man. Denise followed her suit, leaving Mary alone with her sister and Roger.

Some friends.

Mary sighed, glancing at Roger, who seemed to be focused solely on Mary, while Susan stood quietly, staring off into the darkness toward the river.

"They're kind of jerks," Roger said, his tone sympathetic.

Mary studied the man closely for a few moments—he seemed harmless. "Can you take us home?" she asked, ignoring the sinking feeling in her gut.

Roger sighed. "I can't." He shook his head. "I've had too much to drink to drive safely, but..." He paused. "We can take your sister somewhere and she can lie down for a bit. She should be able to sleep it off in just a couple of hours—then your friends can take the both of you home."

Mary glanced at Susan, and then back at Roger.

I don't have any other option.

We're too far away to walk.

Mary's mind spun, desperate to come up with any other solution for their situation, fear and dread pulsing through her. Unlike most of the *Englischers*, there was no quick call home for help. Who would help them, anyway?

"I guess that will have to work," Mary said reluctantly.

Chapter Eight

Mary steadied Susan, using her body to offset her sister, who was leaning on her with nearly all of her weight. She braced against her, and slowly, they followed Roger. Luckily, he had been able to grab a clean-looking blanket, and it was currently tucked beneath his arm.

"You shouldn't have climbed into the back like that," Mary scolded her drunk sister, her anger fueled by the pure dread she felt about the entire situation. "That was reckless, and you could've gotten hurt."

"You're one to talk." Susan rolled her eyes, stumbling over a stick halfway buried in the riverbank sand.

"Why did you do it?" Mary demanded, grunting as she kept her younger sister from falling.

"The same reason you go out," Susan snapped, her voice suddenly seeming quite sober, despite not being anywhere close to the definition. "I'm tired of being bored."

Mary found herself offended by her sister's words. "I am not *bored*," she argued. "I just..." Her voice trailed off.

I don't even have an answer.

Why am I doing this?

Is it even fun?

Thankfully, Susan was too intoxicated to notice Mary's lack of an answer, but as they followed Roger farther down the riverbank toward a patch of trees, Mary's mind swam with the realization. In the beginning, hanging out with Amber and Denise had been fun, and the things they did were new—exciting, even.

But now—now she wasn't sure what was so fun about any of it.

Alcohol tasted disgusting and made people act stupid.

Tight clothes were uncomfortable and seemed to garner unwanted attention.

What was left of the *Englisch* world that could be considered fun? A car? A cell phone? It all seemed to lead to nothing but trouble.

"I think right here will be a good spot," Roger interrupted her thoughts, pointing to a sandy area just in front of a tree.

Mary hesitated, looking around the dark area and then down at the ground. "Are you sure?"

Roger nodded. "It'll be fine. No one will mess with her over here." He tossed the blanket down, before reaching over to spread it out across the uneven sand. "She'll be fine once she sleeps it off."

Mary took a deep breath; nothing about it felt right, but there was no other option. "All right," she mumbled, helping Susan plop down on the fuzzy blanket.

"Oooh," Susan whispered, running her hand along the blanket. "It's so soft."

Roger chuckled. "See." He motioned to Susan, who was now lying on her side, her eyes closed, continuing to stroke the soft fabric. "She's going to be just fine."

Mary thought for a few moments, considering the situation. It just didn't seem safe. "I think I'll sit here with her," she said, sighing heavily. "Will you tell Amber and Denise to come and get me when they're ready to go?"

Roger's eyebrows shot up in surprise. "She'll be fine," he urged. "You can come back to the party. Don't let your drunk sister ruin your fun."

It's already ruined.

"I think I should just stay with her," Mary sighed, her voice growing a bit sharp.

"You'll draw more attention to her and keep her from sleeping if you stay over here," Roger argued, though his tone remained light. "You'll be able to see her from the fire." He motioned to the glowing fire not far away. "She needs to sleep it off," he added firmly.

Mary swallowed hard, suddenly frustrated with the whole situation. Nor did she know what was best for a person who had drunk too much.

Reluctantly, she nodded and followed Roger back to the campfire. She stood on the outer edge, careful to keep her eye on her sister, who did appear to be sleeping soundly.

"I've been looking all over for you," Jerrod said, trotting up to Mary, whose eyes were still on her snoozing sister.

"She had to help her sister," Roger spoke up, nodding over to where Susan was lying.

"So the other Amish chick was your sister?" Jerrod asked, turning to Mary, who finally ripped her glance away from Susan.

"*Jah*," Mary said, her tone distracted by the guilt and conviction gripping her chest.

"Ah, don't let her ruin your evening," Jerrod said, stepping so close to Mary that his arm brushed her bare stomach. Mary inwardly cringed, abhorring everything about her exposed body. "I'm glad you came," he continued, before wrapping an arm around her waist. "And you look amazing in these clothes."

"Please don't do that," Mary said, breaking free from his grasp around her waist, stumbling into Roger, who was watching the two of them intently.

Jerrod seemed to be shocked, and his tone grew sharp. "I thought you liked me."

"What?"

"You danced with me and," he paused, motioning to the outfit she had on. "You got all dressed up—I thought it was to impress me."

Her eyes widened as she realized the assumptions he had made—and the fact that she was most definitely not attracted to him. Not anymore. "I-I'm not interested," she managed to say, backing away from him.

"Wow," Jerrod snapped. "I guess you just wanted to lead me on then."

Mary shook her head. "That's not what I wanted to do," her voice sounded small and unsteady as she spoke. Her chest tightened with anxiety. Everything about what was happening made her unsteady.

"Ah, leave her alone," Roger said, his tone firm as he stepped toward Jerrod.

"Or what?" Jerrod took a step toward Roger, puffing his chest out.

Mary shrank backward, terrified by the look of violence in the two men's eyes—and all for what? Why were they even getting angry?

"We're going to play hide and seek," a voice shouted over the loudspeaker, jarring the two men apart, and relief washed over Mary. Jerrod shook his head and walked away, headed back toward the main crowd gathering around the riverbank.

Thank you, Gott.

Chapter Nine

"You wanna hide together?" Roger leaned over and whispered in Mary's ear.

She gazed up at him, leaned back to check on Susan, who still appeared to be sleeping soundly—well, at least from what she could see, anyway.

"I s'pose," Mary finally mumbled, seeing that Amber and Denise were suddenly nowhere in sight.

Figures.

"I'm gonna start the countdown," one of the guys shouted above the crowd. "You all better run and hide." The crowd scattered, nearly running over each other, racing to the dark woods. Mary's stomach flipped.

She had played hide and seek plenty of times when she was younger, but never in the middle of the night—or with a bunch of intoxicated people.

"Come on." Roger grabbed Mary's hand, pulling her toward the woods. Mary stumbled for the first steps out of hesitancy but resigned herself to letting him guide the two of them into the woods surrounding the edge of the riverbanks. They weren't far from Susan; although, Mary couldn't see her.

Mary mimicked Roger, crouching down beside a patch of trees and brush. Her calves burned and tingled from the tight jeans pinching her skin.

I hate these.

"So, you're Amish?" Roger whispered, leaning over toward Mary.

She squinted into the darkness, barely able to make out the outline of his round face in the pitch black. "*Jah,*" she said and nodded. "I am."

"Why are you dressed like that then?" he asked, his tone unreadable as he asked the question.

Mary pursed her lips in frustration.

Why is everyone so focused on what I'm wearing?

"I can wear whatever I want right now," she finally said, doing her best to hide her pure irritation. It didn't help that she couldn't see Susan, which was all her mind was focused on.

I need to get back to her.

"I've never seen an Amish girl change how they dress," Roger continued, his voice still low and hushed. Laughter erupted not far from them, and Mary jumped sideway, startled by the sudden noise. Roger chuckled at her reaction. "It's a little spooky out here in the middle of the night, huh?"

"*Jah*, I guess," Mary said, embarrassed by her reaction, but also desperately wishing Roger would just be quiet. "I should probably go check on Susan."

As she began to rise to her feet, Roger pulled her back down, causing her to plop down on her bottom beside him. "You can't leave yet," he said. "If they catch you, they'll make you shotgun a beer."

"Make me what?" Mary asked, her eyebrows shooting up with sudden fear. The only shotgun she knew of had absolutely nothing to do with any kind of drinking.

"It means you have to drink a beer really fast," Roger explained. "Like basically just inhale it and choke it down."

Mary's nose scrunched up in disgust. "That sounds awful," she whispered, wrapping her arms around her knees. The urge to go home was stronger than ever, and she was filled with regret.

I should've never come.

"I'm pretty good at it," Roger said. "But it's a learned skill—just like beer is an acquired taste."

Mary forced a light laugh in the darkness, though every inch of her being was completely miserable, and the worry for her sister's well-being rattled her brain.

Roger scooted closer to her.

She could feel the soft fabric of his t-shirt brush against her bare skin, and the acid began to build up in the back of her throat as she reminded herself of how much of her was exposed in the clothes she was wearing.

How do they wear this kind of stuff and not feel disgusting? Gott, *please for forgive me for being so stupid.*

"I think you're the prettiest girl at this party," Roger suddenly whispered, his hot breath tickling Mary's ear. The hair on the back of her neck stood on end, and she swallowed the bile in her mouth. His arm suddenly wrapped around her waist. "I knew you put off Jerrod because of me. He's a jerk, you know. I would *never* treat you like that."

Treat me like what?

Despite being purely terrified of Roger's arm around her, she suddenly found herself angry—angry at Roger for touching her and angry at herself for even thinking that following him into the woods was a good idea.

"Please take your arm off of me," Mary warned in a low whisper, figuring she would try a softer first.

"I just thought you might be a little chilled," Roger cooed, still whispering right into her ear. "Have you ever been kissed?" His lips brushed her ear.

That's it. I'm done.

Mary jerked backward, shoving Roger off of her. *"Get off me,"* she said, her voice carrying through the stillness of the night.

Roger lurched back, his eyes wide with shock. "Why'd you have to go shoving me like that? That was totally unnecessary," he said with irritation.

"I told you to stop touching me and you wouldn't," Mary snapped, standing to her feet.

"You came with me into the woods—what did you think would happen?"

But Mary was already moving away, sprinting out of the woods to find Susan.

Chapter Ten

"*Gott,* I'm so sorry," Mary whispered as she headed along the riverbank, ignoring the shouts around her. Those who were 'seeking' were chasing those who were 'hiding,' while others were doing what she assumed was shot-gunning beers, liquid running down their faces and soaking their clothes.

Gross.

Just as the blanket by the patch of trees came into her view, she froze, stopping right in her tracks.

Susan was gone. Panic thumped in Mary's chest as she reached the blanket.

"Susan!" she shouted, spinning around, scouring the edge of the woods for any sign of her sister.

Where could she have gone?

Mary's head began to feel light, and the scene around her beginning to go hazy.

Breathe.

Breathe, Mary.

You can't find Susan if you're passed out.

She forced herself to fill her lungs, realizing that in the midst of panicking, she had forgotten to breathe. Her vision cleared and her head steadied, but the terror remained, pounding within the cavity of her chest.

Unsure of exactly where to begin the search, she headed back toward the main crowd of people, surrounding the fire blazing in the night. Her legs burned as she quickened her pace, and despite the urge to run, she knew she needed to look carefully. She took another deep breath as she approached.

"Hey, have any of you seen an Amish girl around?" Mary asked one of the girls, sitting alone in a lawn chair. The girl had long black hair and was wearing black shorts and a red t-shirt. However, she didn't look up when Mary spoke to her.

"Excuse me." Mary poked her shoulder impatiently, as the rest of the crowd surrounding the fire was too intoxicated, leaning all over each other and laughing obnoxiously.

"Oh, sorry." The girl looked up, her dark eyes clear rather than hazy like most of the other attendees. "I zoned out for a sec. What did you say?"

Mary felt a little guilty for her sharpness but repeated herself, this time adjusting her voice to sound more pleasant. "I'm trying to find my sister—she's Amish. She was lying over there." She motioned to the blanket still beneath the patch of trees. "But I can't find her now."

"Oh." The girl's eyes widened. "I haven't seen her, but I'll help you look," she added, standing to her feet and dumping out a cup of liquid.

"Thank you so much." Mary exhaled sharply, grateful for the help.

"I'm Elaine," the girl said, smiling. "Where do you want to start?"

"Maybe over there." Mary pointed across where the punch was in large glass jars, before heading off in that direction.

"What's your name?" Elaine asked, trotting to catch up with her.

"Mary," she replied, her eyes scouring the scene in front of her. The punch jars were nearly empty, and there were only a couple of girls standing around the table—none of them being Susan.

"She's not here," Mary said, exasperated, before spinning around to look in the opposite direction. "I don't know where she could've gone. I've never been here before."

"I've been here more times than I'd like to admit," Elaine said, her voice falling a bit. "Let's go look over there." She pointed to the edge of the woods. "That's usually where everyone goes to smoke."

Mary's stomach dropped. "Lead the way," she said, her voice faltering.

"Your sister is lucky to have someone like you." Elaine sighed, as they walked toward the area she had pointed to. "My parents are divorced—and workaholics..." She paused. "They never even notice that I'm gone."

"I'm sorry," Mary said, feeling a bit of sympathy, but too focused on trying to make out the shadows along the edges of the wood.

"Do you like being Amish?" Elaine asked, the curiosity evident in her tone.

"*Jah*," Mary answered.

It's better than this.

"Do your parents mind you dressing like that?" Elaine asked again, as they finally approached the group.

"They would be disappointed if they knew I was wearing this." Mary sighed, finally looking over at Elaine, seeing the softness in her dark-brown eyes, triggering a bit of guilt for being so short with her. "Thank you for helping me," she added, shooting Elaine a small smile.

"You're welcome." Elaine smiled back, before turning to the group of guys standing along the edge of the wood, blowing smoke into the night. "Have you guys seen the Amish girl?"

"The one that was sleeping over there?" one of them asked, blowing out a puff of smoke, right into the Elaine's face.

"Yeah," Elaine said, and Mary realized she was holding her breath against the smoke.

"I think she wandered out over there," he replied, nodding his head toward the rising embankment, as he took another drag off his cigarette.

Mary's chest tightened, and she hurried off, leaving Elaine to jog to catch up as she began to climb the steepening hill.

"This is so dangerous," Mary mumbled as she glanced over the edge, noticing the drop down to the water's edge.

I hope she didn't fall.

The thought spiked adrenaline in her veins, and she took off at a run, leaving Elaine huffing behind her. Mary narrowed her eyes, doing her best to scan the area beneath the hazy moonlight. About a hundred feet away, she saw a dark shadow, seeming to be lying on the edge, her feet dangling off over the bank.

"Susan!" Mary choked out, running toward the shadow. As she approached, she sighed with relief, noticing the outline of the light Amish dress beneath the moonlight. Susan was laid over on her side, passed out. Mary shook her shoulders roughly. "Please, Susan. Wake up."

Susan's eyes fluttered open, just as Elaine reached them.

"Where'd you go?" Susan slurred, squinting up as Mary pulled her away from the edge.

"I was looking for you," Mary snapped, helping Susan to her feet with the aid of Elaine. Mary swallowed hard as she noticed the straight drop down to the rocks below.

Thank you, Gott, *she didn't fall off the edge.*

Chapter Eleven

"She's so lucky she didn't tumble right into the river," Elaine huffed as the two girls worked together to support Susan's weight, slowly making their way back to the party.

"I did what?" Susan mumbled, her eyes half-closed as she stumbled forward.

"I can't even imagine," Mary eked out, fighting to hold back the tears as she thought of the potential harm that could've come to her sister.

And it would've been all my fault.

"Can you take us home?" Mary glanced over at Elaine. "Please?"

Elaine shook her head. "I didn't drive here." She sighed. "Stan brought me. He's my neighbor."

"Oh," Mary's voice broke, tears falling in defeat. She let them fall, unable to wipe them away with both of her hands holding her sister.

"I bet he'll let me borrow his car," Elaine said quickly. "I usually drive us home anyway if he's been drinking."

"Really?" Mary felt hope surge in her chest. "That would be so nice of him."

"He's right over there." Elaine nodded toward a younger man in a cowboy hat, perched in a lawn chair around the fire, gulping down a bottle of water. "Stan," Elaine called, and Sam jerked his head in her direction, hopping to his feet as she approached.

"What's goin' on?" he ambled toward them, his eyes wide as she took in Susan. "Is she all right?" He gestured toward Susan whose head was hanging down.

"She just needs to go home and sleep it off," Elaine said. "Do you think I could borrow the truck to run them home really quickly? I'll come back and pick you up right after."

He nodded. "Sure," he said, his tone warm. "I'm still tryin' to get rid of the buzz I got goin' on. I don't think I'll be movin' from that there chair." He let out a burp, before pointing to the lawn chair he had just left.

"Gotcha." Elaine chuckled. "Thanks."

"Thank you so much," Mary added, though her tone remained uneven. All she could think about was getting home.

"Do y'all need some help getting her to the truck?" Stan asked, eyeing both Elaine and Mary. "I can help you get her over there."

"That would be amazing," Elaine said, as Stan reached to take her place. Mary felt the load on her shoulders lighten as in one swift movement, Stan swooped up Susan, using both of his arms to hold her. Even being a bit buzzed, he appeared steadier than Mary herself.

"Let's go," he grunted, nodding toward the row of vehicles parked off the riverbank.

Mary and Elaine followed Stan closely, as they weaved through the vehicles parked in no real rhyme or reason. Mary glanced back at the river, realizing how far Stan was having to carry Susan, who appeared to be sleeping again.

Finally, they reached a black pickup truck, and Elaine rushed forward, opening up the passenger door. "We'll just have to balance her in the middle," Elaine said to Mary, as Stan scooted her toward the middle of the bench seat.

"That's fine." Mary nodded, sliding onto the bench seat as soon as Stan backed away. She clicked her seatbelt and gazed over at Susan, whose head was leaned back, resting against the back glass. She nudged her gently. "Are you all right?"

"Mmmm," Susan murmured, opening her eyes slightly. "I'm *so* tired," she mumbled.

Mary sighed as Elaine slammed the driver's side door and turned the ignition of the truck. It roared to life, its headlights splitting the darkness in front of them. Elaine eased it forward, bouncing them over the uneven ground and spinning the tires a bit in the sand.

"Where to?" Elaine asked, leaning over the wheel to Mary to catch her eye.

"Um," Mary thought, trying to conjure up the correct route home. "You'll go down the main highway until you get to Inland Point Road," she directed, noticing Elaine nodding. "Then we live right off of 3340 Road in the small white farmhouse with the barn—about a mile down the road."

"Gotcha." Elaine nodded, her eyes now focused on the asphalt road ahead of them. "I'll get you home in no time."

"Thank you *so* much for helping us," Mary said, tears of gratitude threatening to spill from her eyes. "I don't know what we would've done without you."

"Anything to help a girl out." Elaine smiled over at her before reaching to turn on the radio. A country tune filled the cab of the truck, and Mary leaned back in her seat just as Susan tipped a bit, resting her head on her shoulder. Mary took a deep breath and looked at her sister.

How am I going to get her inside without waking Mamm *and* Dat?

If they were to find out Susan had been driven to the party—and gotten drunk, both girls would be in major trouble.

They'll be so angry.

But I can't carry her inside all alone.

"Umm, Elaine," Mary said, leaning over to catch her attention.

"Yeah?" Elaine replied, turning down the radio.

"I have a change of plans." Mary sighed, squeezing her eyes shut. "We're going to go somewhere else."

Chapter Twelve

Elaine turned the headlights off as they pulled to the workshop, about five hundred feet from the Kauffman house —Isaiah's house. Mary hoped more than anything Isaiah would help, as she already was stunned by Amber and Denise leaving her hanging completely in the middle of such a mess.

"Is this your house?" Elaine asked as she turned off the truck.

Mary shook her head. "*Nee*, it's a good friend's—stay here for a minute." She opened the truck door, shutting it quietly behind her.

I just have to get to Isaiah without waking his parents.

Mary swallowed hard, her heart racing as she walked around the side of the house to Isaiah's window. She knew it was to his room—only because he had once pointed it out when she had visited the workshop with her father. Her heart pinged at the memory. It was then that Isaiah had asked for her to go on a buggy ride with him for the very first time.

And now I'm asking for his help—the same night I turned him down.

Yet Isaiah had never let Mary down, even though she had let him down more than once. Sighing, she picked up a small pebble and tossed it gently at the window. It made a small pinging noise, and Mary bit her lip in apprehension as she waited.

Maybe he didn't hear me.

Just as Mary was reaching down to grab another pebble to toss, she saw a figure appear at the window from the shadows of the room. Her heart dropped.

That's not Isaiah.

It was Samuel, his twelve-year-old brother. Mary gasped at the realization, and she opened her mouth to say something, but he disappeared without even more than a passing glance.

Did he see me?

Should I throw the pebble again?

Is that even the right window?

Mary wrapped her arms around herself, suddenly considering that maybe choosing Isaiah's house was a mistake after all. If his entire family woke up, the mess would most definitely make its way back to her own parents—which would be even worse than had she just woken her parents up in the first place.

Maybe that is what I should do.

Mary's shoulder's sagged as she walked back toward the pickup where Elaine and an unknowing Susan were waiting on her.

Gott, *I am so sorry. Please forgive me.*

She wiped a tear from her cheek as she walked back, preparing herself to tell Elaine they would need to drive back to the original location.

"Mary?" a deep groggy voice said behind her.

She felt another wave of tears escape as she turned to see Isaiah standing in the shadowy yard, squinting at her. His eyebrows shot up as he took her in, before quickly diverting his eyes to the truck parked near a thicket of trees.

"I need your help," Mary choked out, batting the tears from her cheeks. "Susan snuck into the SUV and ended up at the party," she began, before her sobs erupted. "I-I-I…" She sucked in short shallow breaths. "She drank too much."

Isaiah only nodded, heading off toward the truck.

Mary trotted to catch up to him. "I couldn't risk taking her home. I can hardly move her, and I can't imagine the trouble she—we, would be in," Mary huffed.

Isaiah let out a sigh, turning to look at her, his face grim. "We'll put her in the barn to sleep it off, and then I'll make sure to get her home before daylight."

"*Ach,* Isaiah. Thank you so much," Mary said, her voice quiet and thick with tears. "I don't know what I'd do without you."

"Who brought you home?" Isaiah asked.

"Elaine," Mary answered, just as Elaine hopped out of the driver's side, giving him a small wave. "I don't know how I would've gotten home without her. Amber and Denise totally abandoned me."

Isaiah glanced down at her, a shimmer of sympathy flashing, before growing solemn again. "I can't say I'm all that surprised." He grimaced, opening up the passenger side, taking in the sight of Susan. "She's in a bad way," he said, before turning back to Mary. "How much did she drink?"

"I-I don't know," Mary stumbled over her words, fear rising in her chest. "I had no idea she was even there until someone told me."

Isaiah shook his head, exhaling sharply. "I'll keep an eye on her to make sure she's all right," he said, his voice gruff. "Getting intoxicated can be dangerous," his voice came across as chiding and his gaze bounced between Elaine and Mary.

"I'm sorry," Mary whispered, as Isaiah reached across the bench seat, pulling Susan from the cab. She groaned, and

Isaiah shook his head, using his foot to kick the truck door shut gently.

"Will you open the barn door for me?" he nodded to the barn on the other side of the workshop.

Mary waved for Elaine to follow her toward the barn. The two girls got out in front of Isaiah, who was carrying a limp sleepy Susan in his arms. Mary and Elaine pushed the sliding barn door open, and Elaine followed Mary's lead in creating a place in the hay off to the side.

"Thank you," Mary said again, as Isaiah laid Susan down gently into the makeshift bed they had created for her. "Thank you so much," she repeated.

Isaiah stepped backward, gazing down at Susan.

"You're welcome," he grunted, glancing over at her momentarily. Mary swallowed hard at his stiffness. She shouldn't have been surprised by it given the circumstances, but it didn't prevent it from stinging. The cool breeze blew across her bare stomach, and her face rushed with heat. Before that moment, she had completely forgotten what she was wearing.

What he must think of me.

Mary fought the urge to sob again, wrapping her arms around her exposed pale skin. As if the night couldn't get any worse, now he probably thought she was some sort of loose *Englisch* girl.

"I need to get you home," Elaine broke the silence between the three of them. "Stan is waiting on me."

"Of course." Mary nodded, a tear falling down her cheek as she glanced up at Isaiah, who followed them out of the barn and shut the door, his stature stiff as he latched it.

"Thank you," Mary said yet again to Isaiah as the two girls headed back to the truck.

He glanced at her, meeting her eyes, and Mary waited for him to say something. But he didn't.

He turned and retreated back to the house without a single word.

Chapter Thirteen

Mary snuck through her unlocked window, slipping out of the *Englischer* clothes, stuffing them beneath her bed. She'd have to throw them out the next day when her parents weren't around. It was a good thing she had extra *kapps* and plenty of dresses. Otherwise, the missing dress and *kapp*, still tucked away in Denise's SUV would be an obvious loss.

They aren't my true friends.

Her heart ached at a friendship that might as well be considered lost. Their complete lack of care had been disturbing—though looking back, maybe it shouldn't have been. After all, they had treated Mary as though she were a novelty, introducing her to their other friends as the *Amish girl*, rather than just using her name. She swallowed hard, wiping the makeup from her face.

They were never really my friends.

More tears slipped from her eyes, making it that much easier to remove the foundation from her face. If it hadn't been for Elaine, she may have still been stuck at the party, left searching aimlessly for Amber and Denise in abandonment. Would they have even been around to take her home later? The unknown answer made her sick to her stomach.

Everything about the night made her sick to her stomach.

And the fact that Isaiah had been so cold with her.

I deserved it.

She sighed, climbing into her bed. Maybe it shouldn't have bothered her, but it did. Tears ran down her face, dampening the pillow beneath her. She had been the one who wanted to play the field—the one who had chosen a party over a buggy ride, likely ending their courtship. It didn't have to be said for her to know that was the truth.

Yet Isaiah still had helped her, even when he didn't have to.

She squeezed her eyes shut tightly, and her hand shot up to stifle the sob escaping from her lips.

I messed everything up. I'm so sorry, Gott.

She apologized over and over to Him that night, but the remorse and guilt were stronger than ever before, pulling her under in a wave of pure conviction.

I'm never going out again. I'm done with the Englisch *world.*

For her, it had proven to be nothing but pain. If only she had listened to those around her, but she hadn't. There were too many fun and exciting stories that floated around of others enjoying the worldly pleasures of the outside world.

But for her, everything out there had turned out to be nothing but complicated and disappointing.

Her mind flashed to Isaiah's blue eyes, filled with rejection as she had turned him down to go to the party. Mary's heart ached even more deeply, suddenly aware of the feelings she had ignored ever since linking up with Amber and Denise.

I've always loved him. And he would've chosen to be with me.

The thought of what could've been rattled her mind, leading to more intense sobs. Rolling to her stomach, she allowed herself to let loose, her face buried in the pillow. Sorrow and heartbreak filled her as she realized how badly she had let him down. Had it not been the middle of the night, she would've hopped on her bike and ridden back over, just to tell him how grateful she was—and how sorry.

Maybe I can change his mind.

The glimmer of hope was enough to calm her sobs, and she rolled back over onto her back, staring at the ceiling above her. She glanced over to window, still unable to shut her mind off, thinking of how much Isaiah had always been interested in her. Slowly, she convinced herself she could win back.

Sighing, Mary tossed and turned, still fighting sleep, the worry about Susan returning every time her eyes closed. She resigned herself to breathing in and out deeply in rhythm, doing her best to calm her mind.

The minutes felt like hours as they passed, still leaving Mary without a wink of sleep. She drummed her fingers on the quilt before rubbing her fatigued eyes.

I guess no sleep is fair punishment for the mess I made.

She waited, watching the window where she knew her sister would be climbing through at any moment.

Does she even know to come through that window?

Dread filled Mary's mind. She hadn't even thought to open the window in Susan's room. She threw the covers back and slipped out of bed. The last thing she wanted was for Susan to make it all the way home, and then get caught right outside the house because she didn't know how to get back inside. She was grateful their two bedrooms were on the first floor—something she always thought inconvenient as the bathroom was upstairs. But now, it was a different story; she thanked her lucky stars for being on the ground floor.

Mary's door only creaked a little as she opened it, peering down the silent hallway. The entire house was still dark—still asleep. She crept across the wooden floors, stepping lightly and efficiently, careful not to cause any loud creaks. Her father had always been a light sleeper and would hear her even from upstairs.

Susan's bedroom was right next to hers. Holding her breath, Mary pushed the door open, revealing the empty bed. She crept to the window and opened it, but not before peering out into the darkness. There was a slight hue of light beginning to peak above the horizon, causing Mary's heart to drop.

She needs to get home.

A creak startled her from behind, and she spun, terrified of the possibility of seeing her mother or father behind her. Mary let out a sigh of relief as she saw Susan standing in the threshold of the door, looking tired as ever.

"You made it. You must have come through my window, " Mary whispered, her heart filling with gratitude for Isaiah, who had made good on his promise—just like always.

Chapter Fourteen

"Are you feeling all right?" *Mamm* eyed Susan, who was sitting quietly at the table, only hours after returning home—not that *Mamm* knew that, of course.

"I'm fine," Susan said groggily, resting her head against her hands. "I just didn't sleep well at all last night."

"There was an owl outside the window," Mary said quickly, shooting a glance over at her sister. "It kept me up most of the night at well."

"I must've slept right through it." Their mother shrugged, before chuckling. "I think I can just about sleep through anything these days."

Mary forced a fake giggle, but her eyes stayed on Susan. She looked *bad* and Mary was surprised her mother hadn't thought she was sick or at least pressed further into the matter. There were dark circles beneath Susan's bloodshot hazel eyes and her face looked three shades lighter than normal. In the middle of morning chores, Susan had paused to vomit in the patch of trees not far from the cattle pens.

"Are you okay?" Mary leaned over and asked in a hushed voice as their mother disappeared from the room.

"Fine," Susan snapped, not even bothering to look at her.

Mary pursed her lips. Ever since returning, Susan had shut Mary out, hardly saying more than just a couple of words to her. Mary blamed it on the hangover that she more than likely was experiencing for the first time, but there was a judgement in Susan's eyes making it seem like it was something much deeper.

"I'm just glad you're all right," Mary said, keeping her voice light, continuing to ignore her sister's volatile attitude toward her.

"*Jah*, right," Susan quipped, taking a moment to glare at her.

Mary's mouth gaped. "I..." Her voice trailed off as their mother reentered the room, pausing to glance at the two of them.

"Don't you have a buggy ride later today, Susan?" *Mamm* asked, a smile tugging at her thin lips.

Susan groaned. "*Jah, Mamm*, I do," she muttered.

"Why don't you let Mary help you pick out one of your nicer dresses?" *Mamm* mentioned, popping the remainder of a biscuit in her mouth. "She has always had a knack for that sort of thing."

"I can do it myself." Susan sat up, scooting her chair back from the table.

"I'd love to help you," Mary offered. "You can wear my yellow one if you'd like. I washed it this week," she added, doing her best to keep her tone light.

"That would look lovely on you," their mother agreed, her smile growing even wider.

Susan rolled her eyes, and Mary glanced at their mother, thankful she had missed the gesture of disdain. Guilt welled up in her chest as she glanced at Susan, who was disappearing down the hallway.

She learned that from me.

"I'll go help her," Mary said quickly, scooting her own chair back and rising to her feet.

"Do you think she feels all right?" *Mamm* asked, her eyes filling with concern as they met Mary's. "She looks a bit unwell."

So, she did notice.

"Lack of sleep can be quite hard." Mary shrugged, hoping her face didn't give her away to her mother. "I thought about joining the next quilting bee," she added, hoping to change the subject away from the hungover Susan.

Her mother's eyebrows raised. "You will? I thought you didn't have time for such things."

"I think I'll have a lot more free time from now on," Mary said, as she gazed down at her feet.

"Truly?" her mother's voice wrung out in surprise. "I have to say, I'm quite glad to hear that, Mary. I was beginning to worry about you sneaking out at night to join your friends."

Mary's mouth gaped. "You know about that?"

"Of course, I do." Her mother let out a chuckle. "Even your old and gray *mamm* has gone through *Rumspringa*."

Mary smiled, comforted by her mother's soft tone and smile. "I guess I better get back there and help Susan." She sighed, her smile fading.

"She looks up to you," her mother said, her voice growing firmer. "This is your chance to set a good example for her."

"*Jah, Mamm.*" Mary nodded, before heading down the hallway to Susan's room, but not before stopping by her own room to grab the yellow dress she had mentioned.

Some example I've set.

Mary peeked into Susan's room, noticing her sitting on the edge of her bed staring blankly out her window, not even bothering to acknowledge Mary as she entered.

"I brought you the dress," Mary said, her voice wavering as she stepped closer to her sister.

"Wonderful," Susan said tersely, jerking her head toward Mary, her eyes shooting daggers at her. "It'll go nicely with the raging headache I have today."

Mary swallowed the growing lump in her throat. "I've heard drinking a lot of water helps," she said, her voice hushed.

"That would be great." Susan's tone was sharp. "If I could even stomach to drink it—I haven't been able to eat or drink anything since I got up. I feel downright *awful*."

Guilt crushed Mary's chest. She didn't even have any words of advice to give to her sister since she, herself, had never even gotten tipsy. She wasn't even sure how to console Susan, or how to make her feel any better.

"Please just leave me alone," Susan said, her eyes full of judgement and hurt.

I'm the worst sister ever.

Chapter Fifteen

Mary couldn't bear to work around the house for fear of breaking down in front of her mother, and so as soon as possible, she found a moment to slip out the door. If questioned later, she'd simply say she wanted to take a walk or ride bikes or something. Fatigue filled her, but she ignored it, heading straight for her bicycle. There was no use in just lying around for the day—it would only draw more attention to the reason behind it. And since she couldn't seem to make amends with her sister, maybe she would be able to make things right with Isaiah.

She pedaled as fast as she could, the heat of the mid-day sun beating down on her face. By the time Isaiah's house came into view, she could feel her dress and *kapp* dampened with sweat. As she pulled to the side of the road, she shaded her eyes with her hand, searching for Isaiah. She hadn't even considered the fact he likely would be running loads of lumber to those around the community.

As she scanned, she saw a figure appear from behind the chicken coop, and her heart fluttered as she realized it was Isaiah. He looked up at her and she waved at him. He shook his head as he headed in her direction.

"I just wanted to say, thank you, again," Mary said as he approached her.

"Susan could've really gotten hurt, Mary," he said, his tone cold and distant as he folded his arms across his chest.

Mary swallowed, noticing the sweat beads across his forehead, above his dark eyebrows and eyes.

"I know," Mary said, her voice coming out in a whisper. "I don't know how I didn't notice her in the back of the car."

Isaiah didn't immediately speak, and Mary could tell he was studying her. "I don't know either," he finally said, his voice having a hint of irritation.

He doesn't believe me.

"I really didn't know." Mary sighed, wishing more than anything that Isaiah would believe her and act the way he always had before—warm and welcoming.

"I guess you should pay better attention then," Isaiah replied, his jaw tensing, his tone even more chiding than before.

"I don't think—"

"It doesn't matter," Isaiah shook his head. "You should be more careful."

Mary felt the all too familiar lump growing in her throat as she held Isaiah's gaze. Nothing about the way he was looking at her felt normal. He was angry with her—and she couldn't blame him.

"I'm sorry," Mary said, her voice maintaining the guilty tone. "I'm really grateful that you helped—I know you didn't have to," she continued, desperate to break through Isaiah's cold exterior.

It didn't work.

"I didn't know you were wearing *Englisch* clothes now," he said, and his voice faltered for a moment with what sounded like hurt.

"I..." Mary's voice trailed off. Samuel heading toward them. Her cheeks flushed with embarrassment as she realized both of the boys had seen her in inappropriate clothing. "I'm just really sorry," she finally muttered, her voice barely audible.

"Well, it's over now." Isaiah sighed heavily, and Mary looked up at him, her eyes glistening with tears. He held her gaze for a moment, and a flash of something other than judgement appeared for just a second.

Mary opened her mouth to speak, but Samuel made it to the two of them at the edge of the yard. He looked so similar to Isaiah—just younger and his eyes were a shade of green rather than blue.

"You were dressed right strange last night," Samuel said, folding his arms across his chest.

Mary's head dropped, unable to look up at the young boy's gaze. She had *really* messed up the previous night. She wiped a tear from her cheek, before looking back up at the judgement Samuel was shooting her way.

"I'm sorry you had to see that," she said, her tone soft, glancing at the silent Isaiah standing beside him. "I promise you'll never have to again."

"*Gut* to hear," Samuel said, before a grin broke out on his face. "Otherwise, next time I was gonna have to throw a sheet over you," he said, a laugh escaping from his lips.

A small wave of relief washed over Mary, but immediately evaporated as she saw that no such lightness had passed over to Isaiah.

"Anyway..." Mary said, her voice drawing out, as she waited, hoping desperately that Isaiah would ask to see her again the way he always had before.

The moment passed by, and Samuel's gaze bounced between the two of them, a look of amusement growing as the awkward tension thickened.

"Well," he said. "I'll leave you two to finish your chat." He raised his brow, before heading back toward the coop.

"I'll see you around, Samuel," Mary called after him, doing her best to hide the pure defeat thrumming in her chest as Isaiah refrained from saying anything more to her. She swallowed, before turning to him. "I just wanted to come and tell you thanks," she said, repeating what she had initially said.

I sound so dumb.

"Well, okay, then," Isaiah quipped, letting out a sigh that cut Mary's heart right in half. He turned to go.

"I'll see you," Mary said, and Isaiah walked back to the coop, his back to her.

He hadn't asked to see her again. And her heart dropped knowing he wasn't going to. He hadn't even wanted to tell her goodbye.

She mounted her bicycle, and took off down the road, heartbreak gripping her chest in one big squeeze and tears running down her face as she rode as fast as she could back to her own house.

I've ruined everything.

Chapter Sixteen

Two days passed, and Isaiah remained completely absent—not even dropping off the lumber for the barn addition. Instead, a hired hand, Keith, was the one who was doing the running to their house with wood. Sweeping off the porch, Mary sighed as she saw Keith return yet again—waving to her before turning his attention to her father.

Isaiah's avoiding me.

She wasn't surprised—not after the way he'd treated her when she had visited him at the chicken coop. But she couldn't help but wish he would come by. His absence had left her with a sense of emptiness.

Mary focused back on the broom, sweeping the dust off the porch. However, the hum of a motor caught her attention, and she looked up, noticing Denise's black SUV pull up outside of their drive. She glanced around, hoping no one noticed the two girls' presence. She leaned the broom up against the rail and ran to the road. The window rolled down on the passenger side.

"Hey, Amish girl," Amber smiled, handing her a sack. "We thought you might want these." She chuckled, Denise joining her.

Mary pursed her lips, taking the bag from her, knowing good and well it was her dress and *kapp* from a few nights before. "Thanks," she muttered, gripping it tightly.

"Sure thing," Amber said.

"Why didn't you bother to help me Friday night?" she blurted, unable to hide the hurt from her voice. "You knew my sister wasn't supposed to be there, and you didn't even check to see if we were all right."

Amber's eyebrows shot up. "I'm sorry," she said incredulously, laughter escaping from her lips again. "Are we like, your parents, or something?"

"You're *nineteen*," Denise added. "I'd think you can be responsible for yourself."

"I mean," Amber cut in, shrugging. "You seem to be perfectly fine, and I'd assume your sister is, too, right? Nobody died," she added with a laugh.

"*Nee,* nobody died..." Mary's voice trailed off, confused by the complete lack of empathy. She had expected them to at least be a little remorseful about leaving her alone.

"Exactly," Denise quipped. "Anyway," she flipped her dark air over her shoulder. "We were thinking about running a 5k. We thought it might be just the thing for you."

"A what?" Mary's brow creased.

"It's a race," Amber sighed, seemingly annoyed by Mary's lack of knowledge. "We thought since you have to walk and ride your bike everywhere, it would be fun for you."

"Oh," Mary said blankly, completely disillusioned by her two so-called friends.

"Well?" Amber snapped. "What do you think?"

"I think..." Mary paused, steadying her voice to keep from sounding nasty. "I think I don't want to hang out with you anymore." She let out a deep breath.

"Excuse me?" Denise said, taking off her dark sunglasses. "Why don't you want to hang out with us anymore? Just because your stupid sister snuck into a party and got wasted?" Her tone was full of annoyance.

"That's just ridiculous," Amber said, rolling her eyes.

"I've decided that I'm done with *Rumspringa*," Mary said, folding her arms, feeling as though a heavy weight had been lifted from her shoulders.

"Geez," Amber quipped. "Have a good life. Let's go, Denise."

Denise nodded, and Amber rolled up the window—right in Mary's face. The SUV pulled away, leaving Mary standing there. Even though she knew they weren't really her friends, their rudeness jolted through her. They had been nice to her—mostly, anyway. But then, she hadn't always been very nice to them, either.

She sighed, turning around to head back to the porch, so she could finish sweeping it. Glancing over to the barn, she noticed her father staring at her with his eyebrows raised. As they made eye contact, he gave her a slight smile, and she forced one back as she grabbed the broom. However, as she made long strokes, sending clouds of dust off the porch, a cloud of loneliness overtook her.

I have no friends.

My sister is angry with me, and Isaiah doesn't want me anymore.

Tears were becoming more of an everyday thing, but Mary didn't even attempt to hold them back as they once again slipped from her eyes, running down her cheeks. In the entire nineteen years she had spent alive, she had never felt more alone than she did in that moment—and it was all her own doing. If she had only turned away from temptation instead of giving into it. She found herself praying quietly in her mind as she swept.

Gott, please forgive me for choosing the way of the world. I choose to forsake that now. This is where I belong and where I want to be.

Please let Isaiah see the change in me. Please give me a second chance.

Amen

She wiped the dust and tears from her cheeks as she finished sweeping and praying. Whether or not it was God's will for her to be with Isaiah, she wasn't sure, but she did know her realization of love a few nights ago hadn't been just a wave of emotion caused by the gratitude of his help.

It was real.

And all she could do was hope and pray he would be able to see she was truly done with the *Englisch* world and *Rumspringa*. There would be no more parties or cars or skimpy clothing that made her feel uncomfortable and soiled. She was ready to follow God's plan and live according to His Word and her Amish ways for the rest of her life.

And hopefully, that meant sharing a life with Isaiah—maybe even starting a family with him. Her heart jumped at the thought, and a smile crept across her face as she daydreamed of such a future with the man who had only ever been helpful to her, even when she wasn't to him.

Now if only he could see it, too.

Chapter Seventeen

Mary ran her hands along her green dress, smoothing out the few wrinkles that had managed to find their way into the fabric. She had yet to see Isaiah after bidding Amber and Denise goodbye for good, but she knew he would be at the youth singing. She fully intended to tell him that she was there to stay for good.

And maybe that I love him.

But maybe not.

She took a deep breath, pushing a stray strand of hair back in place. Her heart pounded just at the thought of revealing such strong sentiment to him, especially after how cold he had been toward her the last time they had seen each other. However, she'd given him good reason to act that way.

And now she had to give him good reason to change his mind.

She had prayed diligently every single night, praying he might see the change in her. She hadn't had anything more to do with *Rumspringa*, officially bidding it goodbye. Her mind had played out scenarios where Isaiah was happy to see her again, and they were able to restart their courtship.

But she also considered the more heartbreaking alternative of him not wanting anything to do with her. Both were possibilities.

Susan walked quietly beside her as they joined the other youth, and Mary glanced around, her eyes searching for Isaiah.

"Hello, Susan," Daniel Stein appeared from seemingly nowhere, a large grin plastered across his face.

"Hello," Susan said quietly, a blush creeping in her cheeks. Mary glanced at the two of them, feeling a tinge of jealousy. The two had been inseparable ever since their buggy ride— the same day Susan was incredibly hungover. Daniel was Susan's senior by two years, but it didn't seem to bother either of them. The two had served as a good distraction for their mother, too. Neither of her parents had mentioned the absence of Isaiah, but she knew there was a chance they already knew things had ended.

Mary gazed around now that Susan had left her standing alone. Her eyes scanned the crowd before she caught her breath, noticing Isaiah. He was looking more handsome than ever in fresh white shirt and trousers. She drank in his broad shoulders and strong, tanned arms.

He is by the far the most handsome of all the men.

She blushed, just thinking of it. Her chest swelled with pride as she thought of how he had been interested in *her* out of all the girls in the community. He was a catch, and she should've appreciated it long before she did.

Taking a deep breath, Mary took a step in his direction, only to stop, when she realized Isaiah wasn't standing alone. Frannie Lambright was with him, smiling and chatting up at him, her eyes as bright as the sun. A strong pang of jealousy slammed against her chest, and she turned to focus on the rest of the group, rather than approaching Isaiah.

Does he like her?

It was as clear as day Frannie liked him. She could tell just by the way her body leaned in and her cheeks flushed as they spoke. Mary stole glances over at the two as the singing proceeded, and she noticed that Isaiah was smiling across at her often—just like he used to smile at her. She swallowed hard and wrapped her arms around herself, struggling to hide her emotions.

They might just be friends.

She racked her brain, trying to remember whether or not the two had ever been friends before. She couldn't remember, but what she *did* know was Frannie was one of the prettiest girls in the community—and it made perfect sense that someone as handsome as Isaiah would be attracted to such a girl. Frannie had never bothered to even participate in *Rumspringa*, and that fact alone made her seem like the perfect match for the devoted Isaiah.

She's likely a better person than me.

The more Mary tried to focus on the songs, the more her mind continued to tear her down, making her feel worse and worse for the mistakes she had made.

It didn't matter that all of the youth were allowed to partake in such things during *Rumspringa*. It didn't matter that Mary had turned away from it all.

It just didn't matter.

Mary had blown her chance to be with Isaiah, even if he and Frannie were only friends. All Isaiah probably saw when he looked at Mary was one big mistake. She swallowed the lump in her throat that felt like it was choking her, leaving her to only mouth the words rather than sing out the way she used to. As it ended, the youth began to mill about, and Mary glanced over to see her sister Susan heading off with Daniel.

Going for another buggy ride.

Her eyes scanned the rest of the youth, face by face, as they chatted and stood about. She stopped when she noticed Isaiah through the wide barn doors.

He's leaving with her.

Isaiah and Frannie were walking, their arms brushing one another as they made their way toward his buggy, parked not far away. Mary caught her breath, trying harder than ever not to cry right there in the middle of the crowd as her heart plummeted.

I just need to go home.

She started toward her bicycle, leaned up against a hitching post and noticed Susan's missing—more than likely Daniel had stowed it away in his buggy. Mary did her best to keep her eyes focused on the bike, but her glance drifted one last time to where Isaiah was helping Frannie into the buggy. As he turned to walk around and get in himself, he looked up, his eyes meeting hers.

Mary held his gaze, misery creeping over her as she realized there was no affection in his gaze. Reaching up to her face, she wiped away a tear before it ever fell down her cheek.

Gott, *please help me move on.*

Chapter Eighteen

"Can you pass me that hammer?" her father asked, pointing to the tool resting on the ground only a few feet away.

"Of course." Mary scooped it up, passing it to him. She gazed up at the sun, beating down on them even more intensely now that it was mid-afternoon. It was warm—very warm, and she wished for nothing more than a cool glass of water. Sighing, she cast her eyes toward the house, silently praying that her mother or Susan would appear with fresh glasses.

But they were nowhere in sight.

I bet Susan is off seeing Daniel.

The two of them had been courting seriously enough that Daniel had joined the family for supper. He was a nice fellow, but he talked a lot more than Mary preferred—and his jokes weren't very funny, but Susan seemed to think they were. In fact, all Susan ever did was go on and on about how funny Daniel was and how nice of a man he was. However, she still avoided talking to Mary much.

In fact, they didn't talk at all beyond just around the supper table. Mary knew that given time—or the chance to apologize again—things would get better. Until then, all she could do was pray that their relationship would mend, and things could return to normal between the two of them. Susan no longer glared at her or gave her judgmental gazes, and that in and of itself was a victory.

"This is taking a lot longer than I anticipated." Her father grimaced, wiping the sweat from his brow as he hammered in yet another nail. His light hair had gone mostly gray, but other than that, her father hadn't aged much. He was still just as strong as she remembered him to be as a little girl.

"Some things just take time," Mary said, shooting him a smile as she grabbed another framing board.

"You've been quite positive lately." He smiled back at her, the sweat on his face glistening in the sun. "I like this positive Mary."

"Me, too." Mary laughed, helping her father hold the board in place. Usually, she would've been working on quilting or helping with laundry and other odd jobs, but her father's helper hadn't shown up, so today she was working as his hand.

It had been nearly eight days since she had seen Isaiah courting Frannie—and it was only a short time later that it had been confirmed through Grace at one of the quilting bee meetings. Initially, Mary had been heartbroken, crying in her room, and thankfully, her parents had given her the space needed to overcome such heartbreak.

But Gott *is always good.*

Mary had snapped out of it after only a few days of being upset, realizing that she had no choice but to move on, and in doing so, she had discovered she loved her community, serving in any way she could.

"I had to stop by the Kauffman's and order more lumber," her father said, his tone cautious. "In deciding to add the extra ten feet, I didn't have enough."

"I see," Mary said, meeting her father's hesitant tone with a light smile. "When are they delivering it?" she asked, ignoring the fluttering in her chest at the thought of seeing Isaiah. They had run into each other a few times over the last few days, but Isaiah had just come across as extremely uncomfortable—she doubted this time would be any different.

"Should be any time now, I'd think," her father said, his tone losing the air of caution, causing relief to wash over Mary. The last thing she wanted was for her father to think she was still hung up on Isaiah. Her father cleared his throat, eyeing her again.

"What is it, *Dat*?" Mary asked, her eyebrows furrowing at his awkward expression.

"You know the Lantz boy—what's his name?" he began, his voice laced with a bit of embarrassment as his cheeks reddened.

"You mean Luke, right?" Mary replied, holding back her laughter. Courting was never something her father had handled with grace.

Her father nodded. "*Jah*, that's his name."

"What about him?" Mary asked, a smile tugging at her lips. She already knew what he was going to say. She had caught Luke staring at her when she was over there helping his mother hang out her laundry a couple of days before. His mother was widowed, losing Luke's father to a bad case of influenza, and so she appreciated the company and the help.

"He asked about you when I saw him at the lumber yard yesterday," *Dat* began, avoiding meeting Mary's gaze. "He seemed real interested in you."

"I see," Mary replied.

Luke was a nice man, though he was a bit rough around the edges. He worked hard, much like everyone else did, but he was a bit of a flirt—and had courted any girl who would agree to it.

"Do you like him?" her father blurted, his eyes wide.

"Not really." Mary shrugged, noticing they were still holding the same board in place—no nails had been driven.

Her father sighed. "That's *gut*," he said, before chuckling. "I didn't like him much for a son-in-law either."

Mary erupted in laughter, the board slipping from her hands. Her father joined in, and she suddenly found herself happy, thoroughly enjoying the bonding moment she was sharing with her father. It had been a long time since she had felt so at home with her family, no longer restless or tempted by the things that existed outside of the community.

Despite the heartache and her mistakes, joy had managed to creep in, taking her soul by surprise, blessing her happiness.

Chapter Nineteen

Mary hammered one of the nails in herself and stepped back, gazing at her work with pride. Not that driving one nail really deserved accolades, but she still felt a little proud she had succeeded in helping her father.

"Ah, there you are, Isaiah," she heard her father call suddenly. "I was starting to think you weren't going to make it today."

She glanced over, surprised to see Isaiah driving the wagon full of lumber up toward the barn. He hadn't been to their house for a load drop off since things had ended between the two of them.

"Sorry about that. I had quite a few drop offs to make." Isaiah's deep voice boomed across the yard, sending sparks through Mary's chest. She cast her eyes back to the framing in front of her, knowing she still had three more nails to drive in the places marked by her father. Determined to avoid any contact with Isaiah, she continued with her task, pretending like he wasn't there—even though her fingers trembled holding the large framing nails.

"I expected Keith to make the run," her father said, as Isaiah hopped down from the wagon. Mary laughed a little to herself, noticing the curious tone in her father's voice. He had really been fond of Isaiah, so it didn't surprise her he was prying a bit.

Mary found herself lending an ear to Isaiah's answer as well.

"I, uh..." Isaiah began, before pausing. Mary glanced up from her work, meeting his green eyes for just a moment. "I thought I would go ahead and drop them off—it was on my way," he added quickly, though his gaze continued to wander right back to hers.

He's different today.

After everything that had happened, Isaiah *never* made eye contact with her, with the exception at the youth singing, of course. A jolt of excitement pulsed through Mary, but she shook her head, chiding herself for even reacting in that manner.

It doesn't mean anything.

He's probably just becoming more secure with Franny.

Mary let out a sigh, allowing her excitement to be overcome by disappointment, though she was relieved she didn't feel the need to cry this time. Thankfully, God had helped her get in better control of her emotions, even if the ache remained deep.

"Mary," her father called to her. "Why don't you help us unload this wagon today?"

Her eyes widened, and she replied only with a slight nod.

"I can get it," Isaiah said quickly, as Mary made her way toward the two of them standing beside the lumber wagon.

"Nonsense." Her father waved him off. "She's my hand today. John's wife just had her baby, so I gave him a couple days off to sort things out. Mary here," he gestured to her, now standing beside him, "has been just as good as help as any man."

Mary blushed feeling Isaiah's eyes on her, and she glanced up, meeting his stare. She forced a smile, and she hoped he'd mistake the cause of her reddening cheeks to be from the glare of the sun, rather than from standing in his presence.

"All right." Her father clapped his hands together, breaking the tension growing between Mary and Isaiah. "Let's get this wood unloaded."

Mary felt the all too familiar stirring in her chest as she followed the two of them to the wagon. Swallowing hard, she did her best to shove the feeling aside. The last thing she needed to do was go back to falling apart after she had just gotten herself together.

"Here." Her father handed her the end of a stack of wood and placed the other end in Isaiah's hands. "You two carry this over there. I'll grab a stack of my own."

Mary nodded, and began walking backward, struggling to hold up her end of the stack. She was strong for her size, but still not as strong as a man.

"It's nice of you to help your *dat* out," Isaiah said, his eyes focused on her face as they carried the wood to the pile.

"I didn't want him out here by himself," Mary said, her voice shakier sounding than she would've preferred. She blew out a sigh of relief as she set her end of the stack down, wiping her hands on her dress. She could feel Isaiah's eyes still focusing on her as she headed back to the wagon.

Why is he staring at me like that? Do I have something on my face?

Quickly, she used her sleeve to wipe the sweat and sawdust from her face, hoping that if that were the case, wiping it would solve it. However, as they continued to unload the wood, she continued to feel Isaiah studying her. She shifted a bit uncomfortably under his gaze, unsure of his intentions.

Maybe he's just trying to make me uncomfortable.

It didn't seem like something he would do, though. Isaiah had never been one to hold any sort of grudge.

He's definitely not avoiding me now.

They dropped the last bit of wood onto the stack, and she watched as her father shook Isaiah's hand.

"Would you like a glass of water?" her father asked him. "I'll go fetch us some."

Isaiah seemed to consider the thought for a moment, hesitating to answer. "That would be great," he finally said. "It's a hot one today."

"It sure is." Her father nodded. "I'll be right back."

Mary watched as her father headed in the direction of the house to retrieve glasses, and it left her alone with Isaiah, who had turned back to studying her again.

"My *mamm* mentioned you gave one of your quilts to Rachel Zook," he said, stepping toward her.

"I did," Mary said, thinking of the older widow, who was in desperate need of new bedding. "Her fingers are eaten up with arthritis, and she can't sew any longer." Mary shrugged, doing her best to play it off. "I already have a nice quilt, anyway."

"That was right kind of you," Isaiah said, a smile emitting through his voice. Mary glanced up, meeting the eyes she had done her best to avoid. As her heart fluttered, she let the disappointment back in to stifle it.

"I guess you're done with *Rumspringa*," he said, the smile fading from his face, his voice faltering a bit.

Mary nodded, forcing a soft smile. "I am most definitely done with it. I've found my place here," she added, ensuring that her tone stayed light—lighter than his. She wasn't sure why his tone seemed a bit solemn, perhaps because of the bad memories associated with her.

He's courting Frannie.

He nodded, and Mary's heart flipped as she recognized the softness growing in his face toward her. It reminded her of the way he used to look at her.

Before she broke his heart.

"Water?" her father interrupted, passing a glass to each of them.

"This is refreshing," Mary exclaimed, savoring the coolness on her tongue, before gulping it down. She heard both Isaiah and her father chuckle at her reaction.

"I've got to head out," Isaiah said, as her father retrieved the empty glass from him. "Thanks for the water."

"You're welcome."

"It was nice to see you, Mary," Isaiah said, his eyes falling back to hers again.

"You, too," she agreed, her voice growing soft again.

She and her father returned back to working on the barn, but Mary's mind remained stuck on the conversation she and Isaiah had shared.

Even if he was going to court or even marry Frannie, maybe they could at least be friends.

Chapter Twenty

Mary stood quietly at the youth singing, the first one she had been to since recognizing that Isaiah and Frannie were courting again. She stood alone as her friend, Grace, was now officially married and no longer able to attend such gatherings.

Lucky Grace. Blessed Grace.

Mary began mouthing the words as her eyes drifted across the group of her peers. As per usual, Susan was standing as close as she could to Daniel. Mary half expected her to leave the girls' side and wander over to the boys' side.

Being that Susan was only sixteen, she still had a few years before she would be permitted to marry Daniel—the youngest possibility being eighteen, but she didn't see her father going for anything younger than twenty. Susan and

Daniel were growing serious very quickly, and the thought unnerved Mary, sending a bit of worry through her mind.

She has to wait almost four years.

That's a long time.

I'll be twenty-three by then.

And alone.

The thought rammed into her like a ton of bricks. It was something she had never considered—spending the rest of her life alone. Fear rumbled in her chest as the youth around her sang jovially. Mary swallowed hard, doing her very best to focus on the words, singing praises to God. She squeezed her eyes shut tightly.

Gott, *please don't let me end up alone.*

I don't want to be alone forever.

But she couldn't see herself with anyone other than Isaiah, who was clearly seeing himself with Frannie. She glanced over at him, then at her. They kept stealing glances at one another.

Ugh.

Mary shook her head, knowing it would be best if she just didn't watch the two of them. She had made her peace with it and had moved forward.

Even if pieces of her heart hadn't.

As the singing came to an end, Mary was one of the first to head back to her bicycle. She had no desire to hang around with the rest of them, and she grimaced as she saw her sister and Daniel race for his buggy, giddy with excitement. She ignored the pang of jealousy.

"Hi Mary," a voice called after her.

Mary spun around, inwardly grimacing as Luke appeared, his light brown hair peeking out from underneath his straw hat.

"Hi, Luke." Mary forced a smile.

"How're things going?" he asked, shifting his weight from one foot to the other.

"Fine, I s'pose," Mary replied, catching onto his nervousness. She should've felt a bit flattered, but instead felt absolutely nothing.

"Would you like to go for a buggy ride?" he asked.

Well, he doesn't waste any time.

"Actually," Mary said, unsure of how exactly to let him down easy—she had never had to before. "I am quite busy with all of my work," she finally said, noticing Luke's expression drop. She glanced across the grassy area, noticing Isaiah walking beside Frannie, though his eyes were elsewhere.

Looking right at her.

"That's all right," Luke finally said, and Mary tore her eyes from Isaiah. "I just figured I'd try. All the men are pining after you, you know."

"What?" Mary said, her mouth gaping. "I don't think that's true."

Luke chuckled. "You'd be surprised."

Mary pursed her lips, unable to find anything entertaining about what Luke had said, though it did seem to flatter her a little. Maybe, if God willed it, as she continued to try to move on from Isaiah, there would be someone willing to court her —other than Luke, of course.

Mary bid Luke a good night and headed toward her bicycle, and as she stood it up, she noticed Frannie heading right for her.

Uh oh. What could she want?

"Mary," Frannie said, her tone a bit short.

"Hi, Frannie," Mary greeted her, swallowing hard. She had never had any sort of issues with her, but tonight her stomach felt odd in her presence. It wasn't nauseous or nervous, but it didn't feel good—whatever it was that was causing it.

"I was just wondering if your *mamm* could repair some of my *dat's* trousers," she asked, her tone remaining a bit cold, and Mary realized there were articles of clothing draped over her arm. "My *mamm* insisted I ask you."

"Of course," Mary muttered, struggling to comprehend the strange feeling coming over her. Her mother often repaired articles of clothing that were considered unsavable, so it was no surprise that Frannie was seeking out her services. Although, it seemed right odd she would do so at the youth singing.

"Well, here," Frannie snapped, handing over the pants. "You can just have your *mamm* drop them off at our house. There's no need to give them to me," she added, her brown eyes boring into Mary's, causing her to cringe.

Why is she mad at me?

Did I do something wrong?

Frannie nearly tossed the pants at her, before turning away and heading back toward Isaiah, whose face looked absolutely petrified. Mary felt heat flush her cheeks, and she turned away, stuffing the pants into the basket on her bike. She swung a leg over and took off, making sure she didn't glance back in Frannie's and Isaiah's direction.

Chapter Twenty-One

Mary was surprised to smell breakfast wafting down the hallway so early, as she always helped her mother prepare the meal. The only time her mother cooked without her was when Mary wasn't feeling well or had a late night—neither of which applied that morning. Mary stepped into the dining room, just as her mother was setting the bread on the table.

"Why didn't you wait for me to help you?" Mary asked, her eyebrows creased.

"Your *dat* left early this morning for the Lambrights," her mother said, a solemn look on her face. Mary thought back to the trousers she had given to her mother only a few days before. There was no way she had gotten them fixed yet. There was only one other option.

"Did one of their cows get out *again*?" Mary asked, pulling out a chair from the table.

Her mother shook her head. "Frannie and Martha were in an accident yesterday evening." Her tone was even graver than before.

"What?" Mary's eyes widened as her mind began to spin with scenarios. "Are they all right?"

"Well, both are going to be fine," her mother said. "Martha managed to get away with just a fractured arm, but Frannie broke her leg."

"Oh, my goodness." Susan gasped from behind Mary, startling her. "That is just awful. Was it because of a car?"

Their mother nodded. "A truck didn't yield and hit them. It totaled the buggy and killed the horse, but luckily the women survived."

Mary's mind jumped to Isaiah, who was more than likely completely panicked with the whole ordeal. She could only imagine the fear and urgency of experiencing something like that with someone you love.

Does he love her?

She shoved the question deep into her chest—that was the last thing she ought to be thinking of in the middle of a situation like this. Regardless of her feelings, it was only right to lend a hand to those within the community, no matter how snappy Frannie had treated her.

"I'll make a casserole for them," Mary said, looking up at her mother.

"That would be right kind of you." Her mother smiled warmly at her, before turning to Susan. "Do you think you could help me repair these pants for Peter Lambright? I'd like to be able to take them with us when we take the casserole."

"Of course." Susan nodded.

Mary glanced at her younger sister, who seemed to be growing up right in front of her eyes, losing the childish look to her face. Susan was a talented seamstress—just as talented as their mother, and there was no doubt she would carry on the business once her mother decided to give it up.

Mary, on the other hand, wasn't very good with a needle and thread. But she could cook. She was very good at that.

Once she finished up breakfast, she and her mother worked together on the breakfast casserole.

"Did they put her leg in a cast?" Mary asked, as she whisked the eggs.

"I would assume so," her mother replied, her tone a bit grave. She stopped measuring ingredients to look at her, causing Mary to look up from the bowl. "I think it's very kind of you to reach out to her the way you are," her mother said, her tone tinged with a hint of sympathy. "I know that Isaiah courting her can't be easy."

Mary raised her eyebrows. "I-I don't know what you mean," she said, though inwardly she couldn't help but be a bit surprised that her mother was so in tune to her feelings.

"You were heartbroken for days when Isaiah started courting Frannie," her mother said, her tone hushed. "I would understand if you're feeling a bit of resentment toward her."

Mary sighed. "It was difficult," she admitted, staring down into the orangey mixture of eggs in the bowl. "But I know *Gott* will work things out for my life. He's forgiven me for my mistakes while running around with those *Englisch* girls, so I am sure he'll bring the right man along when it's time."

Her mother was silent for a few moments, and Mary knew she was studying her closely. "That was a very mature thing to say," *Mamm* finally said, her tone soft and comforting. "You have come such a long way in such a short amount of time," she added, pulling Mary into an embrace.

"Thank you, *Mamm*." Mary inhaled her mother's sweet vanilla scent, reminding her of all the times she had spent in her mother's arms as a child. "It means a lot that you've noticed."

Chapter Twenty-Two

Mary carried the casserole carefully into the Lambright's home, following her mother and Susan, before setting it gently on their dining room table.

"Thank you so much," Peter Lambright, Frannie's father, said when Mary's mother handed him the freshly repaired trousers. "And thank you for the casserole," he added, sending Mary a smile. "Martha and Frannie are both resting in their rooms," he added. "You're more than welcome to visit with them."

"I'm going to peek in and say hello," her mother told Mary and Susan.

"I'll go, too," Susan smiled, following after her, along with Peter.

Mary stood silently in the dining room alone, though there were other members of the community floating around the house, also there to lend a helping hand. She could've gone with her mother and Susan, but she was nearly certain that Frannie would not be interested in chatting with her after the way she had treated her only a few days prior.

Her eyes searched around, surprised that Isaiah wasn't there. She had prepared herself on the way over, expecting him to be there.

But he was nowhere in sight.

"Mary," her mother said in a low voice, appearing in the dining room again, waving for her to come over.

"What is it?" Mary asked, her brow creasing as she drew closer.

"Frannie asked to speak with you," she answered, an unreadable look on her face. Mary's heart to drop in her chest.

What could she possibly want to talk about?

Letting out a sigh, she wandered down the hallway, making her way to the bedroom her mother indicated. She couldn't imagine Frannie having anything to say to her. They hardly talked, and it was clearly not amicable from Frannie's side.

Mary held her breath as she entered the room, taking in the white walls and Frannie, lying on the bed with a cast clearly visible sticking out from under a light quilt. Her face had a few light bruises, but she still had her *kapp* on—and a scowl on her face.

"Why are you here?" Frannie asked, not even giving Mary a chance to give any sort of greeting.

Taken aback, Mary's eyes widened in confusion. "I b-brought you a casserole," she muttered, stumbling over the words.

"But why?" Frannie asked, her eyes studying Mary, who was now standing, wringing her hands in front of her. "Why are you being nice to me?"

Mary bit her lip. "I don't understand…" her voice trailed off. She had never been one for confrontation, and she usually avoided it. She definitely would've not come had she known Frannie was so angry with her.

"Don't be innocent," Frannie continued, ignoring Mary's obvious confusion.

"I'm not," Mary said, exasperated. "I don't really understand why you're so angry with me," she added, her voice trembling a little.

"It's obvious you still love Isaiah," Frannie accused, her face scrunched in frustration.

Mary froze at her words, her mind beginning to spin as a lump gathered in the back of her throat.

Is it that obvious?

She hadn't thought anyone had known of her true feelings for Isaiah—maybe her mother, but definitely not Frannie. Mary had done her very best to be respectful of their relationship and hadn't even spoken to Isaiah much, except when he brought lumber over to their house. Was that when she had done something wrong? She racked her brain but was startled by Frannie speaking up again.

"You don't have to lie to me about it," Frannie said, her voice suddenly faltering, hurt breaking through her snideness.

Mary gazed at her, recognizing the pain of rejection in her eyes. "I'm so sorry." Had Isaiah done something? Had he broken up with Frannie?

A tear slipped down Frannie's cheek as she held Mary's gaze. "Just admit that you still love him, Mary."

Mary hugged herself, wishing so desperately it wasn't true. She didn't want to hurt Frannie—or Isaiah. If she admitted to such things, it could potentially ruin their courtship—if it was still going on.

"Tell me the truth," Frannie pleaded, a few more tears rolling down her cheeks. "Please."

"I..." Mary hesitated, pursing her lips and trying to swallow her nervousness. "I do still love him, but..." she said, doing her best to steady her tone, "it doesn't mean anything. He is courting you, not me."

Sobs escaped from Frannie, echoing in the room, causing Mary to cringe and take a few steps backward.

"I'm really sorry," Mary said, her voice thick with sadness. "I didn't mean to cause any trouble at all, I promise."

"You just don't get it, do you?" Frannie cried, her face falling into her hands. In that moment, Mary wished more than anything she could disappear, fading into the white of the walls, and not be the reason Frannie was crying. She had only been trying to right her own path, not destroy anyone else's. It broke her heart to see Frannie sobbing.

"I'm sorry," Mary whispered, though she still didn't understand exactly what was going on here.

Frannie's sobs quieted, and she looked up at Mary. "He still loves you," she said, her voice low and broken. "He loves *you*."

Mary's eyes widened, and her stomach twisted, leaving her stunned. She didn't know what to say, and she could only stare at Frannie, who was now shaking her head at Mary's silence.

"It's true, Mary," she said, looking back up at her. "I'm no fool. I *know* he loves you."

"I…" Mary started and then stopped, having nothing to say. She could hardly even think. Nothing about what Frannie was saying made any sense. Isaiah had clearly not shown any interest in her whatsoever. How could he love her?

Chapter Twenty-Three

Mary sat on the edge of her bed, still unable to think straight. Her hands palmed the quilt around her, desperate to fidget with something. Her stomach felt nauseous, and she had skipped out on lunch, heading straight to her room. The conversation with Frannie had left her rattled, and she hadn't been able to make much conversation with her mother or Susan on the ride home. Thankfully, neither had pried into what had happened, for she wouldn't have known what to say.

He still loves you.

The words echoed, spinning round and round in her mind, making her feel light and excited, but also absolutely terrified.

It made no sense.

And it's wrong to be happy about something that makes Frannie so sad.

She shook her head, looking out across the yard to the barn. Ever since the night of the party, Isaiah had acted so distant toward her, distant *and* cold. There was no way he had loved her anymore at this point—maybe before, but not after she had rejected him. It wasn't until the day at the barn that he had shown any sign that they *might* be able to be friends.

But even that seemed like a reach considering he was clearly courting Frannie, and their past was anything but smooth.

But he did stare at me a lot. That doesn't mean he loves me, though.

It doesn't necessarily mean anything at all.

Mary dropped her head into her hands, fighting the urge to cry, sucking in a deep breath. There was no use shedding any tears about it. In fact, there was a good chance Frannie was just worked up and a little traumatized by the accident. That made more sense than Isaiah still having feelings for her. The accident had been petrifying, and she had heard that sometimes trauma affected people in strange ways. So, it could be nothing.

But it could be everything.

"Mary," Susan knocked on her door, before opening it a little.

Mary glanced up at her sister, surprised to see her—she never visited her room anymore. "What is it?" she asked.

"Isaiah is here asking to speak to you," she said, her voice a little quiet. "I think it's pretty urgent."

Mary swallowed, her nerves swelling in her chest. "All right," she said, her voice faltering as she stood to her feet. Susan nodded, ducking away from the door.

"Wait," Mary called after her, and Susan stopped, turning around.

"*Jah?*" she asked, her eyebrows raised.

"Can we start again?" Mary took a deep breath. "I know I was an awful example, and I am *so* sorry that I let you down and broke your trust. I should've been better."

Susan's lip trembled as she gazed at Mary. "Of course, we can," she said as a tear slipped from her eyes. She wiped it away. "I've been wanting to talk to you—I didn't know what to say, you know? I know I wasn't being smart that night either."

"It was all my fault," Mary said, her voice firm. "Don't blame yourself. I should've been a better example, but I'll make up for it."

Susan smiled at her. "You better get out there and talk to Isaiah before *Dat* chats his ear off," she said, laughing a little. "We can talk later."

Mary nodded and let out a sigh, her heart pounding in her ears as she walked through the house to the front door. She saw her *mamm* and *dat* standing on the porch with Isaiah, and when she opened the door, she could hardly breathe.

"We'll let the two of you talk," her father immediately said, taking her mother gently by the arm, squeezing past Mary. The door shut behind them, and Mary stepped forward, biting her lip as she gazed at Isaiah.

Maybe he's mad at me for upsetting Frannie.

"I just left Frannie's," he began, his tone firm as he gazed down at Mary. She swallowed hard at his words.

Jah. He's angry that I upset her.

"I—"

"She broke up with me," Isaiah cut her off, folding his arms across his chest.

"I-I'm so sorry," Mary said, her eyes falling to her shoes, stunned by his words. "I don't understand why she would do such a thing."

Isaiah dropped his arms and shook his head. "What did you tell her while you were over there, Mary? She was really upset."

"I..." Mary hesitated, looking back up at him. "I didn't tell her anything—nothing. I just took the casserole I made over there and—"

Isaiah let out a deep breath. "She... She told me you were still in love with me. She said you admitted it to her while you were there." He took a step closer to her, invading her space. Mary forced her eyes upward, meeting his pale blue eyes with hers. He searched her for a few moments, and her heart melted beneath his gaze.

"Tell me..." His voice softened, growing a bit husky as he held her gaze. "Are you still in love with me?"

Mary felt the urge to gasp at his words, more aware of him than she had ever been before. The scent of straw and leather filled the air as she forced herself to breathe. Her heart thudded and butterflies erupted in her stomach. She didn't know what to say—or how to say it.

"Frannie ... Frannie told me you still love me," she finally managed to choke out, looking up at him before finally steadying her own voice. "Are you still in love with me?"

A smile tugged at Isiah's lips as he reached out, pushing a strand of blonde hair behind Mary's ear, causing her to flush with heat as she smiled back up at him.

Neither had to answer the questions to know the answers.

Mary let out her breath in a huge sigh, and he gently took her arms and pulled her toward him. She lay against his chest and closed her eyes.

"I tried not to," he whispered above her head. "But it was useless. I love you, Mary, and I always have."

She tightened her hold on him. "And I love you, too."

She pulled back to look up into his eyes. He was smiling down at her. "I guess we're meant for each other."

He chuckled then, the sound rich and warm from deep in his throat. "I guess we are, Mary. I guess we are."

The End

Continue Reading...

Thank you for reading **The Wrong Path.** Are you wondering **what to read next?** Why not read ***Elaine's Engagement?*** **Here's a peek for you:**

Elaine smiled down at her latest embroidery work—a beautiful meadow, dotted with horses and cattle, the golden sun setting behind the rolling hills. There was no doubt in her mind that Doris would display this piece on one of the front shelves of her tourist shop. Of course, this was just what Elaine pictured in her mind, as she had never actually been there. She felt a tickle in the back of her throat and fought the urge to cough.

Ach, *please not again,* Gott, *please. I just got well.*

"Elaine, don't you think you should rest for a bit? You've been toiling all afternoon," her mother appeared in the doorway of her bedroom.

"It's only tiring for my fingers, *Mamm*," Elaine said, sending her a reassuring smile, before adding, "though I could use a walk."

"You've only been well a few days," her mother said and hesitated, her pale-blue eyes filled with concern. "The last time you went for a walk too soon, you fell ill after."

Elaine's own pale-blue eyes dropped to her lap in disappointment. "*Jah*, you're right," she sighed. "I think I'll just finish my embroidery work so *Dat* can deliver it to Doris tomorrow—if that's all right?"

"I suppose so," her mother said, before sitting on the edge of Elaine's wood-framed bed. It was covered in a pastel pink quilt Elaine had sewn the previous winter. It was the biggest sewing project she had ever completed—and it had completely exhausted her.

"You know…" Elaine began, studying her mother's face for a few moments. "I don't see why we must move to Pennsylvania. I'd really rather stay here in Ohio."

Her mother shook her head, a stray caramel-colored lock slipping from beneath her *kapp*. "You'd need to be married to stay. We won't leave you, otherwise."

Elaine watched as her mother tucked the lock back neatly. When she was younger, the elders in the community had said Elaine was the spitting image of her mother, and she was— only much frailer, sicker, and well... Her legs just weren't quite right. Her right leg was a little longer than her left, resulting in slight limp. The *Englisch* doctor had said they could possibly even out eventually with therapy, but any amount of walking just led to more pain and sickness.

"Can't I stay with Grace?" she broke free from her thoughts.

VISIT HERE To Read More!

https://www.ticahousepublishing.com/amish-miller.html

Thank you for Reading

If you **love Amish Romance**, <u>**Visit Here:**</u>

https://amish.subscribemenow.com/

to find out about all **New Hannah Miller Amish Romance Releases! We will let you know as soon as they become available!**

If you enjoyed ***The Wrong Path,*** would you kindly take a couple minutes to leave a positive review on Amazon? It only takes a moment, and positive reviews truly make a difference. I would be so grateful! Thank you!

Turn the page to discover more Hannah Miller Amish Romances just for you!

More Amish Romance from Hannah Miller

Visit HERE for Hannah Miller's Amish Romance

https://ticahousepublishing.com/amish-miller.html

About the Author

Hannah Miller has been writing Amish Romance for the past seven years. Long intrigued by the Amish way of life, Hannah has traveled the United States, visiting different Amish communities. She treasures her Amish friends and enjoys visiting with them. Hannah makes her home in Indiana, along with her husband, Robert. Together, they have three children and seven grandchildren. Hannah loves to ride bikes in the sunshine. And if it's warm enough for a picnic, you'll find her under the nearest tree!